SINKING LOWER AND LOWER . . .

Cold, filthy water flowed around his face and neck and Shane felt himself pulled deeper beneath the Hudson. He could move and swim, and if he could just figure out where he was, he could resurface. And breathe, because right now his chest felt like it was caving in on itself and it was everything he could do to fight the urge to inhale. If he could just—

The hands grabbed him again, pulling at his legs this time, clawlike fingernails hooking his jeans and cutting through the fabric. Then there were more hands, gripping him around his waist, pulling him lower into the water. Slender, powerful arms wrapped around his neck, and he couldn't fight anymore. The cold was seeping into his mind, his thoughts were slowing, darkness devouring his warmth and pulling him down lower and lower into the depths.

And then there was nothing.

THE HOLLOW

BOOK ONE: HORSEMAN

BOOK TWO: DROWNED

BOOK THREE: MISCHIEF

BOOK FOUR: ENEMIES

THE HOLLOW

BOOK TWO:
DROWNED

BY
CHRISTOPHER GOLDEN
&
FORD LYTLE GILMORE

razOr
bill

The Hollow 2: Drowned

RAZORBILL

Published by the Penguin Group
Penguin Young Readers Group
345 Hudson Street, New York, New York 10014, U.S.A.
Penguin Group (USA) Inc., 375 Hudson Street, New York, New York 10014,
U.S.A.
Penguin Group (Canada), 90 Eglinton Avenue, Suite 700, Toronto,
Ontario, Canada M4P 2Y3 (a division of Pearson Penguin Canada Inc.)
Penguin Books Ltd, 80 Strand, London WC2R 0RL, England
Penguin Ireland, 25 St Stephen's Green, Dublin 2, Ireland
(a division of Penguin Books Ltd)
Penguin Group (Australia), 250 Camberwell Road, Camberwell,
Victoria 3124, Australia (a division of Pearson Australia Group Pty Ltd)
Penguin Books India Pvt Ltd, 11 Community Centre, Panchsheel Park,
New Delhi – 110 017, India
Penguin Group (NZ), Cnr Airborne and Rosedale Roads, Albany,
Auckland 1310, New Zealand (a division of Pearson New Zealand Ltd)
Penguin Books (South Africa) (Pty) Ltd, 24 Sturdee Avenue, Rosebank,
Johannesburg 2196, South Africa

Penguin Books Ltd, Registered Offices: 80 Strand, London WC2R 0RL,
England

10 9 8 7 6 5 4 3 2 1

Interior design by Christopher Grassi

Library of Congress Cataloging-in-Publication Data

Golden, Christopher.
  Drowned / by Christopher Golden & Ford Lytle Gilmore.
    p. cm. — (The Hollow ; bk. 2)
  Summary: Shane and Aimee Lancaster and their friends encounter new dangers
in Sleepy Hollow, including cornfield imps and river naiads.
  ISBN 1-59514-025-5
  [1. Supernatural—Fiction. 2. Characters in literature—Fiction. 3. Brothers
and sisters—Fiction. 4. Sleepy Hollow (N.Y.)—Fiction. 5. Horror stories.]
I. Gilmore, Ford (Ford Lytle) II. Title. III. Series: Golden, Christopher.
Hollow ; bk. 2.

PZ7.G5646Dro 2005
[Fic]—dc22
                                                          2005008147
Printed in the United States of America

For my niece, Kasey McGann.
—C. G.

For Harris Miller, who continues to go above and beyond.
—F. L. G.

AUTHORS' NOTE

Local historians in various towns, most of them in Westchester County, New York, have argued for ages about what town or village was author Washington Irving's inspiration for the hamlet featured in his famous story "The Legend of Sleepy Hollow." For years, North Tarrytown, New York, stood firm in their claim as the main influence on the creation of that fictional town. In 1996, the village changed its name, officially, to Sleepy Hollow. If you visit Sleepy Hollow now, you'll see signs everywhere promoting the name and the image of the Headless Horseman, a boon to tourism. Despite the horror of the original tale, there seems something charming about the legend.

For the moment.

Meanwhile, readers who are familiar with Sleepy Hollow, New York (where Golden lived for three years in the early nineties), will notice that while some familiar landmarks are included, many liberties have been taken with the geography of the place.

We won't tell if you won't.

DROWNED

CHAPTER
ONE

THEY HAD EVERYTHING to be afraid of.

The night air was crisp and cool, the moonlight splashing across the autumn-withered field. Glow sticks waved, alcohol flowed, and people danced, giddy with laughter and flirtation. A fire blazed in a hastily dug pit that had been encircled with stones. Music thumped the sky.

Beneath it all there was fear. It was one thing to think about using a cornfield as a party zone but another entirely to use Jim Ingalsby's farm. Ingalsby was out of town, visiting his wife's sick mother. That left a nice dark spot where kids could gather away from the dominion of their parents and actually work at having lives. Steve Delisle was all for a party, but the idea that Jim Ingalsby might come home and find them on his property was a little unsettling. Nothing like a shotgun full of rock salt to kill a party buzz. Steve smirked at the thought and blinked a few times to get his contacts wet enough to stay in place. They were a constant annoyance, but they beat glasses.

So there it was, the tangible fear. Beyond that was the intangible. Not much more than a month earlier there had been several murders in Sleepy Hollow. Gruesome decapitation killings, in which the murderer had done his best to take advantage of the local legend of the Headless Horseman, the image that adorned shops and signs and the banner of the local newspaper. Sick. There hadn't been another murder since, but the town was still holding its breath.

Intangible fears. Whispers about ghosts and haunted trees and ugly little monsters roaming the woods. Sleepy Hollow was a town rooted in superstition, a place where old myths had become an integral part of the community's self-image and economy. But when people started thinking these things were more than superstition, it wasn't fun anymore.

That was Steve's attitude. Nobody wanted to talk about the things they were really afraid of, so they'd rather risk the tangible, dare to piss off Erin Ingalsby's dad with a party in his cornfield.

And here they were. Music, dancing, too much beer, and maybe a little something else besides. Steve was definitely in the partying mood. He had a roll of bills—none of them very large, but they added up—in his pocket to help him score a few party favors. Nothing hard-core, just a little home-grown to smoke.

He scanned the crowd, trying to spot the new kid, but Shane was a no-show. Not really a surprise, but disappointing. Shane Lancaster desperately needed to lighten up. Either that or he was going to drop from a heart attack in the next couple of years. That was Dr. Jekyll's official opinion. Kids had been calling Steve Jekyll since freshman year, when he'd first started hanging out with Mark Hyde. Considering the size and violent reputation of Hyde—currently sitting on the truck's open tailgate and nursing his fourth beer—and Steve's straight-A record, the nickname was sort of inevitable.

Jekyll glanced back at Hyde, who took another sip from his beer and glanced around the field. Hyde had finally gotten up the nerve to ask out the girl he'd been lusting after for the last couple of years, but he was fidgeting because she still hadn't shown up.

A pickup truck sat at the edge of the clearing in the field, music pumping from its sound system and spotlights illuminating the partiers who had gathered there. A second truck and seven cars completed the perimeter, and Mark had commandeered the tailgate of this truck in order to be close to the beer supply in the flatbed. No one was going to fight him for his seat, but he was always good enough to move aside when they reached for another brew.

Jekyll and Hyde chilled at the rear of the truck, watching the crowd. Several couples vanished into the rows of late-season corn to have a little private time. Jekyll was amused, but also a little jealous. He would've liked to have someone to slip off into the corn with.

Hyde let out a sigh. "She still isn't here."

"Yeah, I know." Steve spoke softly. "It's early yet, bud. Life does not grant our every wish."

Mark snorted, his voice a low grumble that meant he was slowly sliding into agitated mode. "Now and then would be nice, dude. It doesn't have to be *every* wish, just one now and then." Steve had no useful commentary on that, so he focused instead on the cluster of girls dancing to the loud trance music blaring from the speakers on the larger pickup. Most of the farm had been harvested already, except for the pumpkins and late-season corn. No berries this time of year. It was a simple enough thing to get onto the property and take up strategic position so that the last acre of corn blocked a view of the party from the house or from any street. The trucks had hammered down a path into the corn and created their very own crop circle, inside of which was the party. The Ingalsby farm was really perfect for their needs. The cornstalks kept them hidden, and the distance from anyone else, even the closest farm, meant the music wouldn't draw undue attention. Ingalsby was going to lose a few stalks of corn, but that was a small price to pay for their rave.

Hyde cracked another beer and took a long swig. He glanced around again. "Crap."

Jekyll smiled, trying to lighten the mood. "Mark. Chillax. Seriously. The more you worry, the angrier you get. The angrier you get, the more you want to wipe out every living thing on the planet. There will be no hulking out tonight. The girl you want to see might not be here, but there's no shortage. See?"

Hyde grunted again and shifted on the truck. The grunt wasn't an answer so much as a concession. There were plenty of pretty girls in the field, dancing and laughing and just generally breaking the hearts of the guys in attendance. Missy Stern, for instance. But none of them was Kimmie Hill, and so the scary look stayed on Hyde's face. That was bad. It made people nervous. Once upon a time, before Steve had decided to change the course of destiny, Mark Hyde had been on his way to becoming a legendary bully. The sort of beast that would have been whispered about by generations of kids instead of just his own classmates. Jekyll and Hyde had been working very hard to remove that particular stain from Mark's past and remake him into a human being that people could actually look at without cringing in fear. Hyde was a giant. Six and a half feet of hard muscle, covered in a pair of black jeans and a T-shirt that advertised the latest Cradle of Filth CD.

Steve was almost a foot shorter than his best friend, thin and hyperactive and smarter than just about anyone else he came into contact with. It wasn't a question of being cocky or full of himself. It was just true. Sometimes it sort of sucked. So Steve had gotten into the habit of mouthing off a lot. Mark was pretty much the only thing that kept him from getting into a fight every day. Steve could handle himself—he had been taking karate lessons since he could walk—but fighting wasn't his thing. He liked not having to do anything with the lessons. It was one of his goals in life.

"So, where's Shane?" Mark's voice was calmer now.

"No-show again."

A moment later the night became a lot more interesting. Stasia Traeger walked into the clearing with Shane's sister, Aimee, who sported a Day-Glo cast on her left arm. Stasia flashed a sultry grin in their direction.

Steve couldn't help grinning in return. The air seemed ten degrees hotter whenever Stasia was around. She moved like a predator and dressed to thrill. The tough girl, and unique. Totally peerless.

6

Not only was she not part of any clique, she regarded those who were as though they were some alien race. But that didn't keep her from partying with whomever she pleased, regardless of their place in the caste system of high school.

As Aimee and Stasia walked over to them, Mark slid off the back of the truck's tailgate and smiled.

"Look, Hyde," Steve said, arching an eyebrow, "dessert just got here."

Stasia playfully bumped a hip against him and smiled. "You wish."

"Why, yes, I do." He grinned at her and then winked at Aimee, who was looking just a little puzzled by him. That was normal. She was a lot like her brother in some ways. She might like to party harder than him—assuming that Shane had ever been to a party that didn't have paper hats and a pony—but brother and sister both had that thousand-yard stare, as though they were observing everything around them from some remote location. Steve thought maybe it was just the shock lingering after their mother's death back at the beginning of the year— the reason they'd moved from Boston to begin with. Or maybe he was overanalyzing it. It might simply be new-kid-in-town syndrome.

"Hey, Aimee," Steve said, smiling broadly.

Aimee looked a little uncertain, but she smiled back. "Hey, Jekyll."

"So, where's your brother tonight?"

"Where else? At home. He never does anything."

"Hey, I've been trying to drag his ass out of the house, get him to socialize. I'm going to have to add more incentive." Steve jerked a thumb back toward Mark. "Maybe if I threaten him with Hyde?"

Aimee rolled her eyes. "Good luck with that." She patted Hyde's washboard stomach and reached past him, grabbing a beer. "Everyone knows that Mark is really a teddy bear."

Hyde blinked. He started to blush, not saying a word. Steve let her have her delusions. That was the idea. He wanted people to remember that Hyde was actually a nice guy and forget about his history of kicking the crap out of his peers for fun.

Stasia slipped past Hyde and grabbed a Sam Adams for herself. She said something under her breath to him that increased his blush substantially. Her smile was known to cause guys to crash cars or trip over their own feet. The two girls half walked and half danced into the deepest part of the crowd, the lights from the other pickup truck illuminating them and almost making Aimee's bright pink cast glow.

Neither Mark nor Steve danced. It wasn't part of their repertoire. Steve turned to Hyde. "What did Stasia say to get you so bothered?"

"None of your damn business." Hyde still looked

8

a little flushed, and Steve had the good sense to leave well enough alone. At least his friend seemed a little more relaxed now.

Steve spotted Bill Hastings and patted the money in his pocket. "Be right back. I crave a little herbal remedy."

Hyde nodded and looked around, his brows knitted together over his broad nose. In the dim light he sort of looked like a lion. A hungry lion with a bad attitude. Steve knew a few girls who thought Hyde was sexy as hell, mostly because he was dangerous as hell. As far as he knew, Kimmie Hill wasn't one of them, but Steve kept that to himself. He wouldn't want to be the one to dash the big guy's hopes.

Bill Hastings had been sampling his own stuff again, but he was still sharp enough to deal fairly. Jekyll said goodbye to his money and hello to enough weed to keep him grinning for a week or two as long as he didn't go overboard. He didn't smoke a lot. There were burnouts he knew who were high all the time, eyes moist and rimmed with red even from first period Monday morning. Steve thought they were morons. But he did like the high life once in a while.

He was just moving back to where Hyde was waiting and brooding when the truck's lights went out and the music stopped. The sudden darkness and the abrupt silence made him freeze and glance quickly around. *What the hell was that?* After a few seconds a couple of the kids around them started grumbling and a few of the girls giggled nervously.

Steve frowned. He'd seen the setup a little while ago, had helped make sure it was all just so. Even if the truck's battery had died suddenly instead of fading slowly, the stereo should have been going strong.

"Look out, kiddies!" somebody shouted. "It's the Headless Horseman!" A small spattering of tense laughter followed the announcement.

"Friggin' Weiss," Hyde snarled in the gloom. Obviously he'd recognized the voice. "I swear that kid pisses me off every time I see him."

Stasia's sexy rasp carried through the darkness. "Heel, Mark."

Hyde would have bruised or broken anyone else who'd spoken that way to him. But he and Stasia were friends, in their own way, recognizing each other as mutual forces of nature. Hyde's response was a noncommittal grunt.

Evan Gosling moved toward his truck. "Anybody messed up the truck, I'm gonna kick some ass."

People started growing less amused and more annoyed as the silence stretched on. Stasia's voice came clearly from the largest cluster of interrupted partyers. "Put your hand there again, Pete, and I'm going to break your fingers."

Even in the dim moonlight Aimee's cast stood

out. She and Stasia came closer and Steve smiled. Hyde struck a match behind him and lit a cigarette. He didn't smoke often, but he did when he was getting edgy in a crowd. Steve started to reach for the joint in his shirt pocket but stopped when the noise cut through the darkness.

It wasn't a human sound. It seemed like it came from a flock of crows, loud and raucous and mocking, taking flight from the limbs of an ancient tree. It was like it was coming from everywhere at once, echoing across the field. A few people let out anxious mutterings, high-pitched and afraid. More than a few of them were guys. Barely a month had passed since the last decapitation, and somewhere out in the woods there was still a tree that whispered secrets and promised hints of the future. Sleepy Hollow hadn't really been the calmest place lately.

Steve heard Mark's steel-toed boots hit the ground behind him, the truck he'd been sitting on creaking as he stood. That wasn't good.

Hyde spoke in a low rumble. "That's it. I'm kicking the shit out of someone."

"Chill, Mark," Stasia said. "It's just someone being stupid. Don't let them get to you."

That unsettling sound—like freakish laughter— stopped as quickly as it had started, leaving everyone spooked and a void where the noise had been that the whispered conversations didn't fill. Steve felt the hairs on his arms and neck rise. If someone was playing pranks, they had taken it as far as they should.

Just as that thought went through Jekyll's head, someone ran very fast through the cornfield just beyond the clearing, knocking aside the full stalks and cackling that damned weird laughter again. Everyone's eyes had adjusted to the darkness by now, but whatever was moving in the corn was hiding very well, too well to be seen clearly.

Then Missy Stern began to scream.

"Oh my God!" Aimee shouted.

Steve looked over just in time to see Missy fall flat on her face. Something had grabbed her by the ankles and was hauling her back into the corn. Her fingers dug and scrabbled at the ground, leaving trenches where her nails bit into the earth as she was dragged deeper into the corn.

The sounds began to spread, the corn rattling from a dozen different directions, and it was clear there wasn't just one asshole out there—not just one bogeyman—but a bunch of them. Kids started backing away as fast as they could, clustering in the middle of the clearing. Aimee took one step in Missy's direction before Adam Weiss slammed into her from behind and spun her halfway around. Steve reached for her, but too late. She swore loudly and fell to the ground, landing on her cast. Her profanity faded into a scream as the wounded arm struck the ground and was pressed under her. Steve looked for Missy but couldn't see anything aside from her thrashing shape as she vanished into the corn.

As Steve dropped into a crouch, reaching for Aimee, he saw Hyde brush past Stasia and set off across the clearing at a gallop, charging toward the place where Missy had disappeared. But it wasn't enough for Hyde to help Missy. Adam had pissed him off twice tonight—first with his idiotic comments and then by slamming into Aimee—so Steve wasn't at all surprised by what happened next. As he thundered across the clearing to deal with Missy's attacker, Mark stuck out his arm and slammed into Adam. The kid lifted completely off the ground and came close to doing a full somersault before he hit the earth.

Hyde ran toward the spot where Missy had disappeared. Steve figured the good news was that she was still screaming. But that was also the bad news, because it meant something in the field was hurting her, or trying to.

They all watched as Mark went in after her, crushing corn down into the soil as he moved. Not far away a second girl let out a shriek and one of the jocks at the party added his own wail of terror. Both of them were pulled into the field around the party spot, even as the laughter grew louder.

"What the hell's going on?" Aimee cried.

"Not a clue. Except someone's going to get thrashed in a minute." Jekyll grabbed her around her middle and helped her stand, surprised by how light she was. "You all right?"

Aimee made a soft mewling sound as she gathered her legs under her. Her face was pale, and he wondered if she'd done more damage to her arm as she fell down.

"I'm fine, thanks," she said. Her eyes were clear and alert and Steve swallowed his worries about her.

Kids were running everywhere now, and Steve pulled Aimee out of the way as the corn in the field shivered and rattled maddeningly. Other than the moonlight and a couple dozen glow sticks, the field was in darkness. Steve reached into his pocket and pulled out a lighter as someone else almost ran into him and Aimee. He shuffled around so any impact would hit him first. Over in the spot where Hyde had disappeared, they heard a loud roar and Aimee jumped. Steve stayed exactly where he was. He knew the sound well enough from the few times he'd heard and seen his best friend really lose his temper in the past. There was angry and then there was nearly berserk. Mark had reached the latter. Something in the cornfield let out a shriek that would have been suited to an alley cat in life-and-death combat and then came the sound of it moving away, crashing through the corn.

The stereo in the back of Evan's truck suddenly blared to life and then the truck itself lit up. The sudden light didn't make the pandemonium any less. Three kids were on the ground, one of them flat on her back and unmoving. Not far away Marty Hodstedder was holding his throat and coughing, his face red and his eyes wide and teary. The last one was just starting to stand up.

Mark came bursting out of the corn, knocking the stalks down under his heavy tread, carrying Missy like she was a puppy. Missy was crying and her shirt had been shredded along with the skin under it in a couple of places. Mark scowled, his mop of hair scattered across his brow and his nose bloodied. He didn't look angry anymore, just confused. Steve understood how he felt. Mark set Missy on her feet and hurried over to him.

"We need to get the hell out of here *now!*" Hyde snarled.

Stasia had been checking on Adam, but now she ran over to them. "What are you talking about? It's just some seniors screwing with us or something."

Something flashed across Hyde's face just then, and Steve felt his mouth go dry and his chest tighten. For just a moment it looked to him like Mark Hyde was afraid.

"What is it, man?" Steve asked quickly, eyes wide, shaking his head. "What are you not saying?"

Hyde's nostrils flared. He clenched his fists and glanced around at the three of them. "Look, whatever's out there is pissed off and it bites! Now, we need to get out of here. Move!"

"Oh, no," Aimee said, and her voice sounded very small. Her face was even paler now, and Steve didn't think it was from pain.

Stasia said nothing, but she gnawed her lower lip and glanced around at the corn.

They moved, heading back toward the road, with Mark leading the way and a small army of kids trailing behind him. Those with cars started them up as the field came alive with the heckling laughter of the things hidden in the rows of corn. Steve looked back just in time to see someone gun the engine on Evan Gosling's truck and slew mud around as he started forward. The truck fishtailed and spilled half of Evan's stereo system out of the back, then it caught hold of the ground again and rocketed out toward the edge of the cornfield. Jekyll pulled at Aimee and called out to Stasia and the others to get to the side just in time to avoid becoming roadkill.

The next car in line avoided the slowdown by ramming through part of the field, knocking the cornstalks down. Evan's truck, however, stopped for a second as something under it crunched wetly under the front tires. Steve stopped moving and watched, half blinded by headlights, as the truck rose and fell back to level ground, crushing something under its weight. He pulled Aimee aside again as the truck accelerated hard and fast, spraying mud and corn behind it.

"Steve? What?"

"Just wait. Just wait right here, damn it." His voice was barely above a whisper. "Look at the truck coming—can you see the driver?"

"Steve, you're squeezing too hard." He eased up the pressure from his fingers, letting blood back into her arms as the truck rocketed past, narrowly missing another kid as it shot ahead of them. He couldn't see who was driving, and he so wanted to.

"Did you see, Aimee? Did you see who it was?"

"No. The windows are up. What's wrong, Steve?"

"I think someone just got run over." His voice cracked. Jekyll's voice didn't crack much, not even in the throes of puberty, and, contrary to most rumors, he actually had gone through his growth spurts already. "I think maybe someone's dead."

CHAPTER
TWO

SHANE SAT IN the living room, looking over a thick sheaf of papers on the sofa next to him. He chewed at a stick of celery smeared with peanut butter and studied the notes he'd written all over his spiral notebook. *Acephalos.* The word was everywhere, spelled in a dozen different ways. He tapped his ballpoint against the page, watching the dark spatters of ink mark the doodles and notes crawling over the lined paper.

His dad was sitting a few feet away from him, doing his own paperwork and setting up stories and articles for the *Sleepy Hollow Gazette*. It wasn't the first time in his life he realized he and his father had a lot in common, including work habits. He probably wouldn't have noticed now, but his dad kept looking over at him and frowning.

When he couldn't take it anymore, Shane finally spoke up. "What, Dad? Do I have a massive pimple on my nose?"

Alan Lancaster smiled at him. "Not that I can see. What? I'm not allowed to look at you now?"

"You're not allowed to keep making that frowny face when you do. Makes me feel like I'm about to be in trouble for something." He scowled. That was the sort of expression his dad normally reserved for Aimee.

"I'm not making a 'frowny face'; I'm thinking."

"So spill it. What's wrong?"

"I'm trying to figure out why my son hasn't been out of the house in the last three weeks."

"I go out every day, Dad." Shane sighed and set down his pen. He'd known this conversation was going to happen. It wasn't completely new, especially since they'd moved to Sleepy Hollow. Shane was sort of a loner. By choice mostly, but even more than usual in the last few weeks.

"To school and to work." His dad shook his head. "I mean really go out."

"I don't feel like going anywhere. Why is that a problem?"

His father set down his own paperwork. It was time for *the talk*, and Shane was going to have to sit through it whether he liked it or not. "Shane, you're too young to not like the idea of going anywhere, especially on a Friday night. You're supposed to be out getting into a little trouble and hanging out with your new friends." Alan stood up and walked over to him, and if he noticed when Shane closed the note-book, he didn't say anything about it.

"I just have other things to do right now, Dad."

"Have you *made* new friends, Shane?" There it was, the old concern.

"Yeah. I have friends." He looked down. "I just don't feel like going out and partying." He made himself grin. "I figured with Aimee around, that would make you happy."

"Come on, Shane. Talk to me. Tell me what's going on."

He knew he wasn't going to get away until he conceded, so he finally said, "Maybe I'm trying to avoid someone."

"A girl someone? Or a guy someone?"

"Oh, definitely a girl."

His dad nodded. "Stasia?"

"What?" Shane half jumped out of his seat. He'd been careful not to let his feelings for his sister's best friend show. Or at least he thought he had.

"Is it Stasia?"

"How? I mean, I didn't say it was. . . ."

"Shane, I'm a reporter. I watch people for a living. What makes you think I'm not going to notice that you run to your room every time you even think she might show up?"

"Well, I wasn't exactly trying to be obvious, Dad." His skin felt too tight.

"Like I said, I'm a reporter. I notice human nature in action." His father shrugged and then pushed Shane's notebook back a bit so he could sit on the couch next to him. "And let's not kid ourselves, Shane. You aren't exactly a master of subterfuge. All anyone has to do is mention Stasia and your ears prick up."

"Let's just keep that between us, okay? I don't need Aimee coming down on me for liking her best friend. The last time that happened, it cost her a friendship. I don't think she'd be real happy with me. And we've got kind of a truce going lately, trying not to snap at each other so much."

The truce hadn't stopped them from arguing, but it did seem to have cut down on the amount of petty sniping between them and the number of full-blown fights they'd had recently.

"Your secret is safe with me, on one condition," his father said.

"Which is . . . ?"

"Get a life. I don't care if you join the chess club, but I don't want you hanging around the house all weekend obsessing about the Horseman killer." Alan blinked, as if hearing his own words and rethinking them. "Look, I know you must be shaken up. Trust me, I certainly am. Especially since the guy is still out there somewhere—"

"Maybe," Shane interrupted. "But I don't think

he's still around *here*, do you? I mean, otherwise why stop? No, I think he's gone."

He hoped he'd put enough conviction into it.

His father nodded slowly. "I hope you're right. In fact, I think you probably are. But even so, I'm still on edge, and I didn't get nearly as close to him as you did. You're my son, Shane. I'm allowed to worry. And part of that is, as long as you keep your eyes open, I really think you should get out more. Staying inside all the time like this . . . it isn't healthy."

"The thing is, most of the people I hang with are in the same crowd that Stasia hangs with," Shane said. "I can't hang out with them unless I want to be with Stasia and Aimee. Aimee's okay as sisters go, but she's not really on my list of weekend buddies."

"Make new friends." It wasn't a request; it was an order. "I mean it, Shane. I don't want you turning into a hermit."

"I'll work on it."

"Good. Then I expect you to be out of the house tomorrow night." He grabbed Shane's notebook. "And actually try doing something that doesn't involve researching the Headless Horseman, okay? I know you said you want to know all the legends of Sleepy Hollow and I guess I can understand that, but try going out to a movie or something."

"I said I'll work on it." Shane's voice was a bit

sarcastic and he knew it, but his father was trying too hard.

"Look, Shane, I know I'm a pain in the ass, and I know you aren't off getting yourself into trouble. Believe me, I'm very happy about that. But I also think you need to remember that whatever you do, you're going to run across Stasia Traeger from time to time and you need to either confront your feelings about her or just get over it."

That said, his father walked back over to his own work. Shane stared for a few seconds, knowing that his father's heart was in the right place and also knowing that if it were anywhere near as easy as his dad made it sound, his life would be much simpler. Nothing was that easy. Not his social life, and not figuring out what was really going on in the Hollow, what might happen next.

There was more to his research than just wanting to know all the local legends. Washington Irving had written in his classic story "The Legend of Sleepy Hollow" that the area where the story took place had a reputation for strange occurrences. That was an epic understatement. What Shane and Aimee had learned was that Sleepy Hollow was cursed and that their own ancestor, Ichabod Crane, was responsible for that curse. The Headless Horseman was real, not just some story.

They'd managed to stop him from killing them,

but it had cost Aimee a broken arm and several people their lives. They had arranged a kind of truce with the Horseman, but Shane was sure he had seen him once, and the whispers continued. The Headless Horseman still rode the wooded hills of Sleepy Hollow, and even though he hadn't killed anyone else, there was no way to tell whose side he was on now.

Ichabod Crane had summoned all kinds of evil things to the Hollow in those days. Now they'd been unleashed again, and Shane wanted to know what else might be out there. He wanted to be prepared for whatever might come their way next. Someone would have to stop the creatures when they made themselves known, and even if Shane didn't think he and Aimee would be able to manage it by themselves, they had to try. No one else would understand what they already knew. Who would believe it? The affair with the Horseman had proved that very nicely. The local police and the national media had all gone a little crazy with the beheadings that had taken place, and the police were still looking for a serial killer. Even after Aimee and Shane had *seen* the demon in action and up close, the adults had insisted that someone wearing a costume was doing the killings. They'd chalked up what the siblings had seen with their own eyes to little more than hysteria.

So Aimee went on like nothing had happened—

and she went on with Stasia, who Shane was trying very hard not to obsess over—and Shane took care of trying to be prepared.

That didn't leave a whole lot of time for partying in the cornfields. Especially if it meant partying with the girl he wanted to be around more than anything. They'd shared one kiss, the night the Horseman had broken Aimee's arm and almost killed them all. They'd danced around it since, but they hadn't out-and-out talked about it. And with every day that passed, it seemed more awkward to even think about having that conversation. All that was left was the uncomfortable glances they gave each other from time to time.

Stasia. Just thinking about her was dangerous.

It was safer at home. Much safer.

But damn, it was lonely on a Friday night.

October was the time for things to start getting colder in New York State, so Gary Barnes bundled himself up a little more and leaned back against his truck. He stared out at the waters of the Hudson River, hoping against hope for a repeat performance of last night, when he'd seen a woman swimming in the moonlight. Naked. He was sure of it. Gary didn't consider himself much of a romantic, but he could easily fall for a girl who looked that fine.

He popped the ring on his second beer of the

night. The air was cold and the water looked nice, but so far there were no naked babes swimming around for his entertainment. He was pretty much of the opinion he wouldn't see her again anyway. That would be like winning the lottery twice. The thing was, Gary was always an optimist. He figured if a girl could skinny-dip in this weather, either she was drunk or she was just crazy enough to be fun.

He finished his beer and threw the can into the river, watching it float and bob along as it slowly filled with water. Then he got the paint cans from the back of the truck. Now and then there was a little left over when he was done with a job, and it was either dump it here or pay to have it disposed of properly. Legally. He preferred to dump the leftovers in the river. It was fun to watch them cloud the waters and disperse. And it was free.

Tonight he painted the waters bloodred and sky blue. A stupid combination, in his opinion, but that was what the client wanted, and as long as they paid on time, he had no problem with what colors they chose to use. The swirls of pigment expanded and spread over the water, and he grabbed another beer as they drifted on their way to the sea or wherever the hell they went.

He thought about staying longer to see if his swimming friend showed up, but there wasn't time. He had to get some quality drinking done and then he had to get to sleep. He had to start on the Stevenson job first thing tomorrow, and there was a lot of work to be done in that place. Too many angles for such a small house.

Back to the truck and out of the cold he went, starting the engine and listening to the first few lines of an old Led Zeppelin song. He was just about to pull away from his favorite dumping site when he caught the movement from the corner of his eye.

There, near the water. Gary grinned, watching in a slight stupor as the girl he'd seen the night before climbed out of the river and walked in his direction. She was even prettier than he'd remembered, with long graceful legs and a muscular body. Her hair was wet and covered a few of her finer features, but that was okay. She was walking right toward him and she was as naked as the day she was born. Why she wasn't half frozen was beyond him, but if she needed any help warming up, he had a few ideas.

Gary stepped back out of the truck. He saw more movement and flicked his gaze past her. A slow smile spread across his face, and Gary knew he had to be dreaming. There were more women coming his way, all of them just as naked as the first one and every one of them as beautiful as an angel. Gary looked at each of them, amazed. This was the sort of thing that only happened in the letters sections of his favorite magazines.

The moon hid itself behind a thin veil of clouds, and Gary frowned. The last thing he wanted was to miss a single moment of looking at his bathing beauties. That was all right. They were still coming right toward him.

"Evening," he said, grinning.

He kept grinning as they approached, mesmerized by the way their bodies moved in the near darkness. He was still smiling when the moon came back from behind the clouds overhead.

When he saw the women clearly again, he wasn't smiling. He was screaming.

And then he was dying.

CHAPTER
THREE

MONDAY MORNING AT Sleepy Hollow High was a lot quieter than usual. Most of the students were either just hearing about the death of Adam Weiss or were in shock about the entire thing. It was one thing to hear about a death on the news, quite another to hear about the death of someone you knew.

Shane barely knew who Adam was. He had seen him around the school from time to time in the few weeks he'd been at Sleepy Hollow High, but he couldn't recall that they'd ever even spoken. Adam was just a kid with short red hair and braces and a goofy grin. Kind of funny and nice enough, at least from a distance.

And now he was dead.

Shane had had more than enough of death lately, and not just because of the Horseman. It had only been the previous winter that he and his father and his sister had buried his mother. Isabel Lancaster's death had been slow in coming and almost a mercy for her when she finally passed. The cancer had devoured her a little at a time. She had suffered a great deal of pain and Shane's father had been there to suffer through it with her.

And God, what it had done to Aimee. She'd grown so bitter, and she'd lost a ton of weight because the idea of eating anything heavier than a cracker seemed to make her ill. When Isabel had been really failing, near the end of her life, their mother had said things to Aimee she never should have—Shane still didn't know the extent of what had gone between them—and Aimee had been badly hurt. He was sure his mom had been struggling with so many different things, and maybe she was just trying to shock Aimee into taking a more responsible approach to life. But in the end Aimee had been torn between anger and grief, and afterward, that had only made it worse for her, knowing that her last days with her mother had been tainted.

And Shane? Well, he was coping. Sometimes. Sometimes he sat in his room and listened to the silence of the house long after he should have been asleep and waited to hear his mom call out. At least that was happening less and less as time went on.

People who hadn't experienced death up close liked to fool themselves into thinking that the survivors could recover from that kind of loss. But it was going on a year since his mom had died, and

Shane had long since realized how wrong those people were. The ache of that loss subsided some, sometimes disappearing almost entirely, only to come surging back when he least expected it. And it wasn't going away. He was resigned to that. He'd learned the hardest of life's lessons, and it wasn't something he could unlearn.

Now, somewhere in town, he knew another family was learning that same lesson. Adam Weiss was dead, just like that. Snuffed out and gone, and nothing in the world was going to bring him back. Shane didn't want to think about the dead kid, but every person he saw was walking around with that same someone-just-hit-me-in-the-stomach look that he'd seen a hundred times in the mirror, the one that still snuck up on him when he wasn't looking. There was a memorial at the edge of Ingalsby Farm where people—mostly high school kids—had left flowers and pictures and notes. Shane had heard about it but not seen it, and he had no interest in going by there.

As irrational as it was, he wanted to hate Adam Weiss for dying and making him remember his own pain. He'd done so much to hide it, and now it was all back.

He shook his head, pressing his lips together. It was stupid—it didn't make any sense at all. Just a few weeks ago he'd been surrounded by deaths and hunted by a thing, by a monster that wanted to take his head off, and he'd been okay through that. He'd been terrified but kept it together. Somehow he'd managed not to think about his mom too much or let anything slip through his defenses—well, maybe Stasia, but that was different—and he'd held it together, and now some kid he barely knew had him falling apart.

"You okay, Shane ?"

Jekyll's voice threw him. He'd been so lost in his own little world that he hadn't noticed his friend coming. "Yeah, I'm good." The lie came easily. He'd been lying for a while now when it came to how he felt. Some things were too personal to share.

"Normally this is where I'm supposed to rag your ass for not making it to the party, bud, but this time . . . maybe staying home was a good thing. You know?" Jekyll's voice was husky with emotion, and Shane realized that though Steve was hiding it better than a lot of the students, he too was affected by the death of Adam Weiss.

Shane looked away quickly, feeling a flash of guilt for not having been there. He hadn't really planned on showing up at the party, but he'd told Jekyll he would try to make it. Another lie. He wondered when it had become so easy to lie. They weren't malicious lies, just convenient, but that didn't make him feel any better about them.

"Sorry."

"Don't 'sorry' me, okay? Just come next time. And with that many people around, I figure you'll survive being around Stasia."

Shane cringed. Just a couple of weeks back Steve had gotten onto the topic of girls—one of his favorite subjects—and had pressed Shane about whether there was anyone he was interested in. When Shane couldn't come up with anyone, Jekyll started naming names. The second he mentioned Stasia, he had obviously seen something in Shane's expression, and that led to a grilling that ended with Shane telling the story of what had happened with Stasia, though he'd changed the location to avoid getting into talking about the Horseman.

At the time it felt easier to just spill the truth than withstand Jekyll's continued harassment to hear it. Now he wished he'd never admitted his feelings.

"It isn't 'cause of Stasia," he said, knowing how weak that sounded.

Jekyll nodded, obviously not believing a word of it. He started to say something but shut up fast when Aimee appeared from the flow of people moving through the corridor. Shane was happy the guy had enough sense to be quiet. The last thing he needed was her hearing anything about what had happened with Stasia. Even thinking about it gave him a flash of guilt. He should have been looking after his little sister, not falling for her best friend.

He knew it wasn't completely rational, but he still blamed himself for her broken arm. Any way he looked at it, he hadn't been there when she needed him. He'd been doing things behind her back that would have caused a whole different sort of trouble if she found out.

"You okay, Aimee?" Steve asked.

Aimee nodded, but she looked ready to explode into tears. Shane knew his sister well enough to know that perception was false, but it still sucked to see her like this.

"I'm okay." She moved closer, her books in her right hand and clenched tightly to her body. "It's just . . . I don't know. I barely knew Adam, but I think he was a nice guy, you know?"

"He was." Jekyll looked at her for a second and then past her, his eyes not really seeming to focus on anything at all. "He was a really nice guy. Hyde's tearing himself up about what happened."

"What? Hyde? Why?" Shane asked.

Aimee sighed. "I thought I told you. Adam knocked me on my butt—totally by accident—when those idiots started pulling their stupid stunt in the cornfield. I think Mark panicked. He sort of came to the rescue and blitzed Adam."

"What? He doesn't think it's *his* fault, does he?" Shane hadn't been there, but he'd heard almost a complete blow-by-blow, and it was pretty obvious

Hyde wasn't responsible for what had happened to Adam.

"No, no." Steve waved a hand. "He just knows he wasn't very nice to Adam." His voice lowered. "Adam was always getting on his nerves." He shrugged as if the fault were his own and looked away from both siblings. "Something about Adam just pissed him off, I guess."

Aimee hugged herself. Shane thought her eyes looked haunted. "Well, at least Missy's going to be all right."

"She's scratched up bad, though. Her stomach is all cut up from being dragged across the ground," Jekyll said. "Whoever jumped in Evan's truck and decided to go for a ride, that's who killed Adam. But it wouldn't have happened if it hadn't been for the jerks in the cornfield pulling their stupid prank. Talk is, it was some losers from the college."

Shane stiffened. He didn't want to talk about what had happened to Missy or what was in that cornfield. He saw Aimee's expression darken, and she spoke up before he could cut her off.

"Prank? You were there, Steve. You heard what Mark said. There were things in the corn."

Jekyll looked at his shoes and then glanced away before facing them again. "Hyde was drunk and pissed off and it was pretty dark, Aimee. He was probably just mad he didn't get to stomp anyone.

35

You really think there were, what, monsters in Ingalsby's corn?"

Aimee narrowed her eyes and looked at Jekyll like he had three heads. "Oh, come on—" Shane opened his mouth to interrupt, but before a word could be uttered, the school bell shrieked out a warning that it was time to get to class. "Don't wait for me today," Aimee told Shane over the sound of shuffling feet. "Stasia and I are going job hunting." Her eyes lowered a bit. "And to pay our respects."

"Respects?"

Aimee didn't answer; she'd already bolted, swallowed by the surge of students moving toward their first-period classes. Jekyll answered for her. "At the place out where it happened. Lots of people are going over later. It's turning into kind of a shrine."

"Oh." And there it was again, the darkness inside him, welling up and promising to keep him company for the rest of the day. Jekyll went off in search of a classroom and Shane followed suit. By the time the last bell had rung, the hallways were as still and silent as the grave.

They hadn't expected a war, but it looked like one was about to start brewing. Aimee and Stasia stood at the place where already a growing mass of cards, flowers, and teddy bears was accumulating, the spot where the other night they had been having a good time until everything went crazy. Someone had even drawn a remarkable likeness of Adam Weiss and posted it on an easel. The attention to detail was frightening, even capturing the way his eyebrows lifted when he was smiling.

Like so many of their classmates, Aimee and Stasia were dressed for mourning. Aimee had worn black pants and a dark gray blouse today, and Stasia had worn a simple black skirt and a dark blue top. Her hair was pulled back into a ponytail and her usual collection of jewelry was missing.

Jim Ingalsby was dressed for farmwork, his jeans and denim shirt and old fatigue jacket covered with the efforts of his day's labor. He had a broad, weathered face. Right now he was breathing hard and his teeth were bared as he ground them against each other. His hands were loosely clenched in fists, and while he wasn't actually attacking Police Chief Ed Burroughs, he didn't seem all that far from it.

The chief was leaning toward Ingalsby like a demented reflection from some alternate universe. They were maybe three feet apart—both of them red in the face.

Stasia watched the entire thing, her eyes practically alight and that little half smile of hers firmly in place. "Think they're gonna swing?" Her voice was faint but clear enough to hear even over the raging debate.

"No." Aimee shook her head. "They want to, but not in front of us."

"I don't really know if I like the idea of being accused of murder, Ed." The farmer spoke with enough venom to intimidate the average snake. "I'd say that I don't like it much at all."

"I'm not accusing you of murder, Jim. Don't go getting dramatic on me. All I'm saying is you have a reputation for getting a little too eager to protect your farm from vandalism and whatever went down here on Saturday night left us with a dead boy on your property."

"I was out of town! How many ways do I have to say it? I was out of town and looking after Lorraine's mother, for God's sake. I sure as hell didn't hire a bunch of hooligans to scare off partyers, because I sure as hell didn't expect to have any showing up in my cornfield and trashing everything."

"Jim, I don't like this any more than you do, all right? But I have to ask the questions and I have to make sure you were actually out of town."

"Well, you can go ask Dave Van Brunt. He was *supposed* to be watching my place."

Ed Burroughs scowled. "I guess maybe I'll have to do that, Jim. I don't want to, but so far the only excuse you can give me is that you were out of town, and I don't have to tell you how serious this is."

Stasia shook her head. "I swear, it's like watching

two apes beat their chests at each other," she whispered to Aimee, then slid past the two men and walked toward the makeshift memorial to Adam. Aimee followed. The small collection of memorials touched her even more than she had expected. It was nothing but cards and a dozen or so small stuffed animals, with both storebought and hand-picked bouquets that covered the area where he'd been hit, but it was also obvious that Adam Weiss would be missed.

"I wish I'd had a chance to get to know him."

Stasia nodded but kept her mouth shut for a moment. When she finally did speak, it almost came as a surprise. "You would have liked Adam. He was sweet. A little hyper, but sweet."

The argument between the farmer and Burroughs was still going on, but in more subdued tones. It finally broke up when another of the town's police officers ran up to the chief and interrupted, not even bothering to keep his voice down. "Ed! Hey, Ed, they found another one, looks like he drowned, just like in the truck."

Aimee turned her head just in time to see Burroughs take three steps away from Jim Ingalsby toward Officer Tommy Dunfee. Dunfee stepped back hastily when he saw the look on Burroughs's face. Aimee had to strain a bit, but she could hear the man's words as he responded.

"Do you think you could actually tell me things without advertising them to the entire community, Tommy?" the chief snarled. "Sorry, sir. Yessir. Won't happen again."

"Make sure that it doesn't."

The man had to have eyes in the back of his head, because even though she was trying to be discreet, Ed Burroughs turned his head and locked eyes with Aimee, his face set like stone. Nope. Not a happy man. She looked away first and hoped he wouldn't bother her. There had been enough trouble with the police chief since the family had moved to Sleepy Hollow. He'd practically accused her father of using the Headless Horseman as a stunt for increasing the *Sleepy Hollow Gazette*'s distribution at one point. And he'd made it clear that he knew about her past troubles in Boston. After another five minutes of standing in almost perfect silence at the memorial, she and Stasia headed toward town on foot. Neither of them was much in the mood for job hunting, but it had to be done.

Shane did his homework while he manned the phones at the *Gazette*. It was a nice arrangement as far as he was concerned because all he had to do was play receptionist and he was never so busy that he couldn't get his work done. Also, it beat the crap out of his one brief stint working at McDonald's, where every shift meant he got to go home smelling like french fries.

The pay wasn't great, but it was enough to give him a steady cash flow. Getting paid to do his homework worked just fine, thanks.

He was finishing up his math assignment when the phone rang.

"*Sleepy Hollow Gazette*, how may I direct your call?"

"Hey, Shane. It's Tom Dunfee. Can I speak to your dad?"

"Hi, Tom." He glanced into his father's office and saw him looking over the layouts for the next issue. "Yeah, hang on."

Tom Dunfee was one of the most regular callers. Shane didn't know how his father had managed it, but the policeman was about as close to an informant as the *Gazette* had. Most of the information he provided was hardly earth-shattering news, but at least it was better than nothing. It was certainly more cooperation than Alan was going to get from Ed Burroughs.

Today Tom sounded particularly excited. Shane waved to his father and held up two fingers to indicate which line he should pick up. His father nodded and grabbed the receiver, talking softly and picking up his pen almost immediately. Shane watched from the corner of his eye as his father's face got serious and he started scribbling notes.

Despite knowing he'd be in deep trouble if he was caught, Shane listened in on the conversation, carefully covering the mouthpiece of his headset. Rule number one: If you're going to eavesdrop, don't give yourself away with the sound of your breathing.

"Wait a minute, there are two of them now?" That was his dad's voice.

"That's right. Two. The guy found by the river in his truck and now an old man found at his house. His wife came home from having a ladies' night out with her friends and found him. The bed was soaked, and he must have had a bathtub full of water in his lungs, but it wasn't a water bed, if you get my point." Dunfee's voice sounded like a hiss of steam. His whisper was almost comically urgent.

"And no one saw anything at either of the scenes?"

"Well, according to a neighbor over at the house, there were three naked women running around. He didn't tell his wife, but he told me when I asked him if he'd seen anything suspicious." Dunfee chuckled into the phone and Shane frowned. A man was dead and for all he knew the women were involved, and Dunfee was making light of it.

His father's voice brought him back to the conversation he wasn't supposed to be listening in on. "You're saying they were drowned and then had their bodies positioned?"

Dunfee stayed quiet for a minute and Shane could hear the sound of heavy traffic in the background. "I'm not saying anything for sure, because I don't know all the details. But I know this much. There was water on the bed, but the bathtub was dry and so was the carpet. If I didn't know better, I'd think someone brought a hose through the window and made the guy drink half the water tower."

"Okay, what's the address on the new one?"

Shane set down the phone, carefully depressing the hang-up button before placing the receiver back into its cradle. Timing was everything. His father came out of his office a few minutes later, grabbing his jacket as he went.

"I have to run, Shane. There's been a murder and I want to get some answers from the police before they close everything down and head out." He stopped for a second and looked at his son. Shane could see that his father was already halfway to wherever he was going in his mind and getting ready to try to pull answers from the cops on the scene. "It's almost six. Why don't you call it a night and head on home before it gets too dark? I'd drop you off, but I need to be on the other side of town as fast as I can get there. You'll be all right?"

"I'll be fine, Dad. Be careful."

"I always am. And I want you to be careful too. Who would ever have thought this little town would have me more worried about my kids than the big city?" He shook his head. "Just watch yourself. I'll pick up something for dinner. Pizza sound okay?"

"Yeah." Shane snorted. "Like I'll ever turn down pizza."

Alan Lancaster waved as he left the building and Shane started packing up his homework. He'd just finished putting everything into his book bag when the fax machine rang twice and started printing out pages.

The pages came from the coroner's office, about the autopsy performed on Adam Eric Weiss. Shane gathered them together and pulled a paper clip from the small box of them set next to the machine. He walked toward his father's desk and prepared to drop them into the in box. Curiosity got the better of him, though, and he began to read.

For several minutes he stood there, horrified by the clinical descriptions of the kid's injuries and the procedures they went through in an autopsy. He felt a shiver run up his back and a little twist of nausea in his gut.

And then he found something that froze him completely.

The truck had run Eric over, breaking bones and crushing his chest.

But it wasn't the truck that had killed him.

CHAPTER
FOUR

"THIS SUCKS. I swear, there's like no one in this town who's hiring, except for the day shift." Aimee looked at Stasia and scowled. "And there is no way I'm giving up my weekends to work at that stupid diner."

Stasia grimaced. "Listen, I like the idea of working for tips, because I know we could get some serious money with a little flirting, but I don't even think about getting up before ten. And they want us there at six? No way, Jose. Life's too short."

The weather was starting to slide toward cold and Aimee's feet were aching. She wanted to go home, but Stasia had suggested they try a few more places, and Aimee herself wanted some source of cash flow other than begging from her father. Money meant a little more freedom, a fact that Shane was ignoring at his desk job. She didn't know how much he was getting paid, but all he'd actually bought for himself so far was a book about the town's history.

"Hey, look!" Stasia pointed at an old theater situated between a CVS pharmacy and a place that claimed to have good Mexican food and great margaritas. The building had a 1940s feel to it, with an old-fashioned marquee and large windows that were currently soaped over. There was a sign at the ticket booth that said NOW HIRING.

Aimee nodded. "That could be cool." They walked over to the doors that were currently propped open and Stasia knocked before stepping into the place.

Inside, the Capitol Theatre was a disaster. There were rolls of carpeting that hadn't been put out, and the wallpaper had probably last been changed sometime before Aimee's dad graduated high school, but the art deco interior, while in need of a good cleaning, was pretty cool otherwise. The walls had layers to them and curves and slots for backlighting. It was pretty gloomy inside, but someone had either found a few of the recessed lights that still worked or was in the process of replacing them. The air smelled of old dust, new insulation, and paint.

"Okay, this has potential," Stasia said, looking around, a grin playing on her lips. "I wonder if there's a balcony in the theater."

"There is, but it needs structural help before anyone can use it." In the dim interior of the place the woman's voice came to them, and both girls turned to look for the source. The silhouette that approached was lean yet curvy, with long hair pulled under a kerchief. When she stepped closer, they saw that the woman's hair was sandy blond and she was very tanned. Her jeans and shirt were dirty, and she had a few smudges beneath her blue eyes. She gave them a lopsided grin and wiped her hands off on a piece of drop cloth that didn't look too filthy.

"What can I do for you guys?"

"We saw the help-wanted sign and figured we'd see what kind of help you were wanting." Stasia stuck out her hand and introduced herself. Aimee followed suit.

"I'm Ella Cairns," the woman replied. "I own this place, or I will in around thirty years when I'm done paying for it. Right now I'm looking for a few good painters if you know any. I had a guy all set up to work on the inside, but I haven't been able to reach him." She waved her hand around to indicate the faded walls. "I still haven't decided if I'm painting or papering yet, but either way I can't do it all myself." Ella shrugged and looked back at Aimee. "Anyway, I'll need people to run the concession stands in a few weeks when I open up properly and people who aren't afraid of a toilet brush when it's necessary."

Ella seemed horribly distracted by the daunting task ahead of her, but she still radiated a kind of bright energy that gave Aimee a good feeling about her.

"My dad just had his restaurant repainted about a month ago," Stasia said. "I can check with him to see who he used if you want me to." She pulled out her cell phone and started to dial before Ella could respond. Aimee studied the woman, a bit dubious. "So how much toilet scrubbing are we talking about here?"

"I'm not expecting a stampede, but you never know, and I don't need anyone working for me who won't actually work."

"Well, as long as there are rubber gloves involved . . ."

Ella grinned. "Oh, yeah. Rubber gloves and an apron if you want it."

"What kind of hours?" Aimee asked.

"Some weeknights, some weekend nights, but not every one of them. It wasn't that long ago I was your age, and I know that actually working gets in the way of living. I can be flexible if I get enough people here." Ella took the kerchief off her hair and shook her head to get her hair where she wanted it, sort of. She was pretty under the smudges, but quirkily so. There was something almost old-time Hollywood about her, and Aimee thought she suited the movie palace very well.

"Okay, now the big question. How early do you open this place in the daytime?"

Ella chuckled. "Not before noon, even on the weekends. I'm a night bird. I don't do mornings."

"Very cool."

Stasia came back over with a number and name written in her tight script on a small piece of paper. "My dad swears by these guys. He says they'll treat you right."

"You're a lifesaver." Ella looked at the paper and carefully tucked it into her jeans. "I was getting ready to lock up for the day—why don't I treat you guys to a soda and we can discuss the details?"

"So we're hired?" Aimee was surprised but pleased. The place had potential and she could definitely see herself working a job with no morning shifts.

"Probably. Definitely if you can agree to what I can pay."

Stasia and Aimee exchanged a quick smile and followed the older woman as she headed toward the door. "Sweet," Stasia said as they walked. "I like movies."

Shane paced around as he waited for Aimee. She was later than he'd expected and he was a little worried. There were things he wanted to talk to her about before their father got home.

To keep himself from wearing a hole in the carpet, he sat down at the kitchen table and picked up his notebook and pen. Homework was done, but the remains of the battle still lingered on the Formica surface. He shifted to a blank page in the spiral pad and started drawing pumpkin faces. It was almost time for Halloween, and weird damned town or not, family tradition said they'd each be carving a jack-o'-lantern in a few weeks. He might as well get a head start on what his would look like.

He'd been at it for ten minutes or so and wasted five sheets of paper by the time Aimee came home. She was smiling ear to ear, and he guessed the job hunt went pretty well.

One look at his face and her smile dropped. "What?"

"What do you mean?"

"What is it you want to talk about? You've got that look on your face again." She walked over and glanced at what he was drawing. He resisted the urge to hide the pictures from her view, irritated that she was already starting in. Like he practiced his expression in a mirror just to annoy her.

"You find a job?"

"Yes. Now stop evading. What's with the look?"

"We agreed we were going to check out the cornfield. Look into what was really scaring people that night," he reminded her. They'd had the conversation earlier that very day.

Aimee shrugged. "No argument. But we also have things to do. You were working. I was job hunting. Look, I get it, okay? Somebody's got to try to clean up after the mess Ichabod Crane made way back when. He's our ancestor, so you figure it's our mess too. I'm not one hundred percent sure about that, but I agree that nobody else is going to just accept all this stuff, so we ought to do what we can. But we have lives."

"Adam Weiss doesn't. Not anymore."

"Adam was run down by a truck."

Shane nodded. "Yeah. He was. But I don't think the car killed him."

His sister stared at him. "But . . . he was alive just before that. I remember because he knocked me over while he was trying to get to the middle of the clearing, away from whatever was in the corn. I know what I saw."

"I don't doubt that. But it's possible you didn't see all there was to see." "Not everything that happens in this town is because of a ghost or a demon, Shane," Aimee reminded him. "Sometimes a mean dog is just a mean dog. And sometimes accidents happen, okay?" She was the one pacing now, the one who looked like she couldn't find a way to get comfortable. "Just because there are . . . monsters and stuff . . . that doesn't mean the ordinary, everyday bad stuff goes away. Yes, there was something in the corn that night. But what killed that kid was a stupid truck with a drunk driver! I was there—I saw it!"

He shook his head. "I have the autopsy report on Adam Weiss." Aimee stopped her rant, shut her mouth, and listened. "The cause of death is being put down as the truck. You're right about that. But they mentioned something sort of weird."

"Yeah, like what?"

"He was found with a cornstalk wrapped around his neck. Not fallen across his neck, but 'wrapped around it tightly, like a noose.' Those are the coroner's exact words, Aimee. Someone or something strangled him with it."

"Maybe he got tangled in it when he was . . . hit by the truck."

"Come on! You don't believe that."

Aimee sighed and hung her head. "Damn it. I hate this stuff."

Shane hesitated a moment, then he nodded. "I know. And I'm sorry to say there's more. Right now Dad's talking to the police about a guy who drowned in his bed. With no water around. And he's the second one."

"Why can't we just leave it alone, Shane? Why do we have to go looking for trouble, like there isn't enough of that already?"

"You know why. You've already said it. We're in this whether or not we want to be. We're stuck with this because of what Crane did." He looked down at his notebook. "If we aren't looking out for the weird stuff, it might come looking for us."

School was boring, as usual. The closest thing to an exciting moment was watching Mark Hyde stare down two of the football players who'd been giving

Steve Delisle attitude. Sometimes Steve deserved the grief he got—mouth as a weapon was still a weapon and everyone had the right to defend themselves— but this time it was like the jocks just sort of forgot that Jekyll came with his own personal Hyde. After the three billy goats gruff caught on that Hyde was staring daggers at them, the fun was pretty much over.

Now school was done for the day and Aimee and Shane and Stasia were walking out to the cornfield again. Aimee couldn't bring herself to get enthusiastic over the whole thing. Her stomach felt like it was filled with a hundred pounds of lead and her head hurt. Stasia and Shane, on the other hand, looked like they were having a fine time. They weren't exactly dancing in the streets or anything, but both of them were excited, like kids anticipating Christmas morning.

The weather was miserable—cold and damp and cloudy enough to hide the sun from sight. Aimee wanted to be almost anywhere else. Up ahead was the place where the last party she'd attended had become a wake, and whatever was responsible for that was probably nearby and maybe even watching them.

"Let's not hang around, you guys. Why don't we just see if we can figure out what the hell's out here and then bolt, okay?" Her voice shook a little, but neither Shane nor Stasia seemed to notice. Well, maybe Shane. He turned and looked back at her for a second, his expression as blank as a clean page in her notebook. She hated that. There were times when he just hid away everything she should have been able to see in him, and she couldn't stand not knowing what he was thinking when that happened. There was a little voice in her head that told her it was probably bad things about her bouncing around in his skull.

That was the problem with having a sibling: most of the time they knew the dirty laundry you were trying to hide.

"We weren't planning a picnic, Aimee." Stasia's voice was casual on the surface, but she was obviously a little spooked. Aimee understood the feeling. Much as she'd like to pretend she hadn't heard them, the sounds of those things out in the thick clutter of the cornstalks had chilled her that night, and the memory of them wasn't helping against the cold now. Her skin was pulling into gooseflesh just as she thought about it.

Shane stopped moving and stared hard at the collection of flowers and trinkets laid out for Adam. He hadn't been here yet. Whatever he'd been hiding before, his expression was now an open book. His eyes were wide and his mouth was pressed tightly shut as he stood before the memorial to a boy he barely knew by name.

Adam Weiss wasn't going to come to school again. He was a closed chapter in the life of Shane Lancaster, or maybe just a footnote.

Just like their mother.

Shane muttered something under his breath and looked around for a minute more, then nodded as if coming to some sort of decision with himself. "So, want to look around?"

"Okay," Aimee said. Stasia looked his way for a second and nodded as well. Shane led the way as they left behind the shrine to Adam and moved into the field proper. "So where was Missy when she got pulled into the corn?"

Aimee walked over to the spot. It was obvious that something had happened there. The cornstalks were broken and trampled, and even now she could see the marks in the dirt where Missy had tried to claw her way free from whatever dragged her into the darkness. "Here. She was right here. And you can see where Hyde went in after her, too." She pointed to the boot marks left behind when Mark plowed into the corn.

Shane reached down and grabbed one of the broken plants, flexing the hard stalk with a little effort. He frowned and shook his head. "Doesn't make any sense."

"What doesn't?" Stasia watched him as he threw down the broken stalk and grabbed one of the unmarked ones, bending the thick green shaft until it cracked and split down the center.

"The coroner's report said he had a cornstalk

wrapped around his neck like a noose." He grabbed the stalk a little lower and twisted it brutally until it broke in three places. "Want to tell me how they made a plant like this bend like a rope?"

Aimee shrugged and wished it was a warmer day. She already felt like an iceberg. "That's what we're here to find out, right?" Even she heard the sour grapes in her voice. She could be hanging out somewhere warm or maybe even doing homework. Anything would be better.

Stasia kicked at a collection of cigarette butts on the ground not far from where one of the trucks had been sitting. Aimee felt a little guilty. Now that the night was done and the party was over, she could see how badly they'd trashed the field. There were tire tracks all over the place, deep trenches carved through the fertile soil, and places where at least one car with an oil leak had lost a lot of fluids. A lot of corn was ruined and there were beer cans, bottles, and dead glow sticks all over the place. She guessed maybe Ingalsby had a reason for being pissed off the day before.

Shane looked like he was going to make a nasty comment, but before he could, the laughter started up. It was the same raucous cawing sound they'd heard the night of the party. Aimee shivered. Stasia looked around fast enough to slap Shane with her hair. Shane had his head cocked like he was trying to identify the sound. He hadn't moved, but he had gone pale.

The corn rustled around them in the nearly windless field. Aimee looked at her brother. "That's the sound," she rasped.

Stasia nodded her agreement.

Then something caught Aimee by the ponytail and pulled her backward. There was a white-hot flash of pain across her scalp and then she was trying to keep her balance as the booming cackle of whatever had her erupted behind her. She flailed her arms around, trying to grab a handful of her own hair to avoid having it ripped out by the roots. "Help!"

"Aimee!" Shane came running with Stasia right behind him. He only made it four steps before he was in the corn himself, and a second after that, something jumped on top of him. Despite the way her movement blurred her vision, Aimee saw the thing land on Shane's back and wrap itself around his body, arms and legs moving in ways that were better suited to snakes than to anything human. He staggered and fell to his knees, trying to reach for whatever had him. Another of the things slithered through the corn low to the ground, weaving with serpentine agility.

Aimee couldn't breathe and her chest ached with the terrified hammering of her heart. She fell backward and hit the ground, her head knocking into the dirt hard enough to make her see stars. When she'd blinked those away, she saw something else. It looked almost like a man. There was a face of sorts with a wide gaping mouth and two eyes, but that was about as close to human as the thing came. It was too thin, too gangly-limbed, like a skeleton almost, but not made of bones.

It was made of corn. The body wore clothes woven from the corn husks and tatters of fabric threaded through the organic material, a shirt and pants and shoes, but all of them looked like they belonged a few centuries in the past. The face was much the same, the wrinkled, dried husks crinkling and rustling as it leered down at her. The thing had hair—sort of—made from the silk from around the ears of corn, and still more of the husks and silk formed the "flesh" of its body. It looked like a scarecrow but with none of the cute trappings of the ones made in craft stores. It was hideous, and judging by the vicious grin, Aimee guessed, so were its intentions.

The cornstrosity reached down and grabbed Aimee with both of the hard cornstalk hands at the end of its freakishly long arms, its fingers digging into the tender flesh of her throat to choke the life out of her.

Aimee started kicking, her legs pulling in tight to her body and then thrusting hard to strike the thing again and again in its narrow chest. Something cracked inside its torso, but it didn't let go. It just kept cawing and screeching as it applied pressure to her throat. The hard stalks that should have been inflexible bent even more and she saw little black suns forming in her vision. She reached with her fingers and caught one of the digits on its palm, bending the cornstalk back until it popped like a firecracker and then hung uselessly. The thing attacking her let out an angry screech and she grabbed a thumb this time, forcing the hard stalk back and away from her windpipe, letting air back into her system as she gasped, her feet still kicking desperately.

She heard Shane cursing under his breath and the sounds of his breathing, strained now and wheezing a bit. The thing standing over her was bent down at an impossible angle, and the grinning face she'd seen before was now snarling but still made the same maddening noises as it tried to strangle her.

Aimee lifted her feet higher and jammed both of her heels into that vile face, pushing as hard as she could with her entire body. The creature strained, then finally let go of her, giving her a chance to breathe.

Shane was on top of whatever had tried climbing over him, and Stasia looked like she was surrounded by more of the things, each as different as a snowflake and every one of them cawing and cackling loud enough to drown out almost every other noise. Aimee headed toward her friend at a run, her vision still blurred with tears and the sudden return of oxygen and blood to her head.

Shane pushed hard at the creature under him, grunting with effort, and was rewarded by a thick cracking sound as its head caved in. That would have been good if it had actually slowed the monster down, but it just seemed to make it angrier. Long sharp fingers slashed at his face, and Shane ducked away just in time to avoid having his nose removed. He got up and backed away as the thing hissed and slithered backward across the soil, pushing into the corn and almost immediately vanishing into the camouflage. The sounds of cackling and laughter grew louder, and Shane backed toward Aimee and Stasia, trying to look everywhere at once.

Stasia was fighting and losing. Whatever the creature was, it had a thick handful of her hair and was leading her around by it while Stasia did her best to stop the torturous pressure on her scalp.

Aimee could see the freakish scarecrows better now and wished she could go back to being half blinded. The one pulling at Stasia's hair had a long beakish nose and the face of a hag and wore a grotesque hat made of corn husks. The thing grinned in Aimee's direction and let loose a loud screeching laugh. Aimee gritted her teeth and hit it with the cast on her hand, praying she didn't break the plaster. The cast held, but the creature was knocked back a little. It shrieked at her in rage.

Letting go of Stasia, it leapfrogged over the girl to reach for Aimee. "Oh, screw this!" Aimee backed away and almost ran into her brother. He used his book bag to knock the corn witch in the face and sent it off course.

Aimee said it first, but they were all clearly thinking the same thing as the corn around them shook and swayed amid the increasing laughter of the demons in the field.

"Run!"

None of them needed any other prompting. They kicked up clods of dirt as they ran hard back toward the open road in the distance. The noise from the creatures actually got louder and the corn shifted, lurched, and rocked with their hidden movement. As they ran on, Aimee saw that the shrine to Adam Weiss was in ruins, torn apart by the demons in the corn.

As soon as they were free of the cluttered field, the cawing stopped. Aimee looked over her shoulder and slowed down a bit, half expecting the things to give chase, but they didn't show themselves.

Stasia was panting, scratched up but not seriously hurt. Aimee rubbed her neck and looked over at Shane, who had an absurd grin on his face. His hair was covered in flecks of corn and a few strands of silk.

Stasia looked at them and smiled. "I think I know what they are."

CHAPTER
FIVE

TWO IN THE morning was a miserable time to work. Roberto Rodriguez would never think otherwise. But it was a fine time for getting a bonus. The man he was dealing with was wealthy, his hands soft and unused to manual labor. His suit cost more than Bobby made in a month, but that was okay. The suit was here to share the wealth, and Bobby never had a problem with that idea.

Bobby worked hard. He owned his own business doing river tours of the Hudson and he made good money—for the few months of the year that people really wanted to take the tours. He declared every penny he earned, both from that little job and from his night shift duties as the harbormaster. In his case the title was pretty much honorary. Not a lot of loading and unloading was done late at night. Well, not legally, at any rate, and his job was to keep an eye out for vandals and also the illegal stuff. He did a good day's work every night of the week except one, and by then he was too tired to do much partying.

The problem was that Bobby liked to spend more than he made. So he set his morals aside for the rich creep, and he smiled and nodded and turned a blind eye to certain activities. Sometimes he even turned that same sightless eye toward his own boat when the situation required it. He just piloted his little *Maria's Dreams* down the Hudson and ignored what happened in the areas where no one could see his passengers doing anything that was maybe a little bit illegal.

It wasn't like it was drugs or murder, just small necessary evils. The price of living in the modern world.

And for that, the man in the expensive suit paid him very handsomely. First he made his usual idle chitchat to hide what was going on, and then he shook Bobby's hand and when he pulled away, there were a few crisp hundred-dollar bills resting in Bobby's palm. Abracadabra, instant money. Today the take was five hundred dollars, which wasn't bad for a start. The rest of the monthly payoff would happen in a couple of days. Never too much money at one time, in case anyone caught on or asked questions.

Bobby made the money disappear and offered the man a cigarette. The old dude never accepted, but

Bobby was raised to be polite. As always, the man waved away the offer with a, "No, thanks, son. Those things will kill you," and went on his way. Roberto Rodriguez didn't know his wealthy employer's name and didn't need to.

Bobby watched until the guy got all the way over to his Cadillac, feeling a small flash of envy. That was a sweet, sweet car.

He counted the money to make sure he wasn't getting screwed over. He wasn't. There was even an extra hundred tonight for a job well done. That made standing out in the cold of October a lot more tolerable.

The night was long, and Bobby believed in doing his work properly. He started his long walk along the riverside pier to check on the few yachts and commercial boats that were stretched out along the way. A quick glance with a flashlight was all he normally needed to make sure everything was in its place. Tonight was no exception. At least not at first.

He was on the return trip down the long wooden walkway when he heard the splashing. Water sprayed up like it was coming from some hard-core waves when he knew that there weren't any. Speedboats and storms made waves, but he'd seen neither tonight. He flashed the beam from his light out onto the water and scanned the surface. There was nothing special to see, until he looked lower still and saw what was beneath the now-calm river.

A woman looked up at him, her hair flowing in the gentle current and her eyes locked on his. She was beautiful, and she should have been half frozen by now. That water was cold and she wasn't wearing a stitch of clothing. Her hands moved at her sides, pushing the water and keeping her submerged.

Bobby looked down at her and shook his head. "Lady, you have to get out of there before you drown."

She couldn't hear him, of course; she was under the water. Motion off to her side caught his attention and he saw a shapely set of legs go darting past. He looked again and a second woman under the waves was turning, arching her body and swimming back, the light hiding most of her as she cut smoothly through the chilly Hudson.

"What the hell are you girls doing?" He didn't expect an answer this time, just felt the need to say the words out loud. They weren't hurt, they weren't drowning, and they seemed perfectly comfortable under the water. And that was about as much weirdness as Rodriguez wanted in his life.

"That bastard slip me some drugs on the sly?" There were plenty of drugs that could be administered through skin contact—at least in the movies—and that made more sense than what he was looking at. People weren't supposed to go skinny dipping in October. He didn't mind the view, but what he was seeing just wasn't normal.

The women looked at him, their faces impassive. And then they descended. He didn't see them swim or make any sudden moves, but they dropped lower into the water, until he could barely make out their naked forms.

"Okay, that's enough. You girls are coming out of there or I'm calling the cops." He went down on his knees at the edge of the pier and shoved the lens from his flashlight right into the water, letting his beam play through the murk and silt of the river to see if he could spot the women a second time.

Something was coming back up, rising too fast for him to focus on it until it finally broke the surface. Roberto Rodriguez watched the nightmare explode from the water and felt its hand grip his skull in a clutch he couldn't hope to break. He never even had a chance to scream before he was pulled into the water.

He tried screaming, tried begging for his life, but the only sounds he made were underwater and the only things that could have heard him were intent on silencing him forever.

"Okay, guys. See if you can follow this." Alan Lancaster looked first at Aimee and then at Shane as he sat down at the dining room table. These days it was getting to be a challenge for all three of them to actually eat together, but Alan was working at home that afternoon.

"What's up, Dad?" Shane asked, and then shoveled a slab of Salisbury steak into his mouth.

"Ed Burroughs is trying to tell me that there's no correlation between the three drownings we've had in Sleepy Hollow in the last week." Alan poured himself a cup of coffee and Aimee took the pot from him, topping off her own cup. "We have a painter who managed to drown in his car, twenty feet from the water. We have a businessman who managed to drown in his bedroom, without so much as a glass of water anywhere around him, and we have a night watchman at the docks who was found with his face in the river and his body on the pier. All three of them dead and two of them in completely dry areas when they died." He sipped his coffee and raised one eyebrow. "Does that sound like coincidence to you two?"

Aimee shrugged. "I might let slide on the guy in the river, but the rest of them sound an awful lot like murder to me."

"Thank you. That's exactly what I said. Burroughs says they were accidents."

Shane shook his head. "What? The guy at home accidentally sucked all the water from the toilet and then ran all the way to his bed before he passed out?"

"Funny thing about that. Our police chief didn't seem to have a plausible answer. He's waiting for something definitive from the coroner's office."

Shane's expression darkened and Aimee remembered how he'd come across his information the other day. "Dad, I put the report on your desk myself, just the other night. I remember seeing it."

"According to Burroughs, he hasn't received the report himself. I offered to fax him my copy. He wasn't very happy."

"Color me stunned." Aimee shook her head in disgust. Her dealings with the police chief had not been exactly favorable. As far as she was concerned, the man was nothing but grief waiting to happen.

"Oh, I'm sure he has his reasons—I can't believe he'd be that dense." Alan shrugged.

"He's trying to hide something." Aimee took a sip of coffee and looked at Shane. "What do you think?"

"Definitely," Shane said. "But I don't know that there's anything sinister about it. Cops hide things from the public. You've got to figure, he's still dealing with one serial killer. If there was a second, he'd look like the most useless policeman ever."

Alan nodded. "Exactly what I've been thinking." He set down his coffee. "No wonder he's being so secretive."

Aimee swallowed her coffee like it was a brick. The last thing she wanted or needed was her dad thinking about the Horseman or any other killers. They'd be under curfew again in no time. She didn't much like the idea of being stuck at home. On the other hand . . . One drowning might be accidental, but three in one week? Not likely. "Well, maybe the deaths are more connected than just through a serial killer. Maybe somebody pissed off the mob or something."

Shane scoffed. "'The mob'? In Sleepy Hollow?"

Aimee was ready to fire off a few snide comments, but her dad beat her to it. "Don't be so fast to dismiss the notion, Shane. There's no rule that says the Mafia is only in the city. Remember, the same Broadway that runs through the center of our town goes right down to Manhattan."

"Well, what do the victims have in common? Do any of them work for the same people?" Shane seemed to warm up to the idea a bit, which was good, because Aimee wasn't in the mood to go looking for any more monsters. They already had to deal with the scarecrow things in the cornfield and she, Stasia, and Shane were also going to look for the Whispering Tree again if they had the time. Ever since the tree had done its best to use her and Stasia as fertilizer, they'd made a point of looking for it from time to time—hoping to destroy it—but they'd had no luck so far. As far as Aimee was concerned, that wasn't exactly a problem, but they still had to try. Unless it had withered and died—wishful thinking and she knew it—that monster was going to kill someone sooner or later. There were still people at the school who talked about it and people who claimed they had seen the tree or had it speak to them.

Her dad pushed back his empty plate and leaned forward. "So we have a potential serial killer. I'm leaning toward some other explanation. Maybe not the mob, but there are reasons other than psychosis that people commit murder. Usually tracking back to money somewhere. Sleepy Hollow isn't exactly the middle of nowhere, but I don't think the odds are good for two serial killers showing up in the same town within a month of each other."

Shane nodded. "Hey, you could really drive Burroughs nuts and suggest it's the same serial killer with a different modus operandi." Aimee knew he was joking by the stupid grin he was wearing, but she still had trouble believing he'd bring up the idea that the Horseman might still be running around.

Alan shot him a dark look. "That's not funny, Shane. None of this is funny. You've both been . . ." He glanced away for a moment, biting his lip. Then he sighed. "I dealt with a lot of unsettling things on the job in Boston. And I'd talk to you two about them because it helped me think and because you're both smart kids. But the violence and the bad guys always seemed to be in a different world from my family. From home. But here . . . maybe it's harder to keep those things apart in a small town anyway, but that's just a part of it. You two have already been way too close to the ugly things this town has to offer. If there comes a day when my own kids are the headline—"

He let the words trail off, looking a little pale.

"We're careful, Dad," Shane said. "We're not stupid. What happened before . . . it was a million to one. Wrong place, wrong time. We're really okay."

"Besides," Aimee said, "I'm not going to have time to get in much trouble. Starting next week, I'll be gainfully employed."

Alan stared at her. "You got a job?"

Aimee smiled. "Don't sound so astonished."

"Tell me."

"That old movie theater that's being renovated? Stasia and I both got jobs there."

Alan contemplated that a moment and then nodded with satisfaction. "That's great, sweetie. It's nice to have some good news for once. I'll have to check the place out."

"It's cool," she said. "And anyway, the point is, you can't worry about us every second of every day.

72

We'll be fine. We have to live; otherwise we might as well just be in prison . . . or never leave the house."

She shot a look at Shane, who pretended not to have gotten the jab.

Alan stood up. "Okay. I get the point. And you're right. I just want to make sure you watch out for yourselves when I can't be there to do it. Yourselves and each other."

Brother and sister exchanged a glance.

"We will," Shane promised, and Aimee nodded in agreement.

"All right. I have to get to the office at some point. I guess now is the time. Thanks for listening."

They said their goodbyes and finished their lunches. Shane took care of the dishes while Aimee gathered her things together; they were supposed to meet Stasia in less than half an hour.

Shane promised himself he was going to save up for a car. His father was using the station wagon most of the time, and walking everywhere sucked. The truth was, the utter uncoolness of driving around in a station wagon pretty much sucked too.

He was walking along with Stasia and Aimee, growing frustrated. The big topic of discussion between the two girls at the moment was their upcoming job at the dingy little theater that was getting refurbished. Shane only half listened. He had a job and he preferred a good multiplex, where the choices were a little more diverse. And with all that was going on, he couldn't understand why they were talking about such trivial things.

When he couldn't stand to be on the sidelines for another minute, he went ahead and opened his mouth. "Okay, you two, enough about the job. Stasia, you were going to do some research and get back to us. Have you figured it out? You said you knew what they were, these things we're facing. So, spill. What are they?"

Stasia's eyes flashed with excitement. "I think they're guardian spirits. From what I could find, they're supposed to be harmless, but once they've been summoned to protect something, they can be very, very persistent."

Shane frowned, shaking his head. "Wait. You think Ingalsby summoned these things? To keep his crops safe? I know the guy has a reputation, but I'd think he'd be a little more hands-on than that. Rituals and ancient spirits seems a little far-fetched."

She laughed. "I'm not saying Mr. Ingalsby did it. I think one of his ancestors might have and now that the bargain made with the Horseman was broken, maybe they just came back to do their job again."

"So it all comes back to that stupid curse." Aimee was muttering under her breath, but both of them heard her.

"Well, yeah." Stasia turned around and walked backward along the shoulder of the road, looking at Aimee. "When the Horseman made his bargain with the town founders, he promised that he would suppress the supernatural creatures in the area. Think about it like some kind of gate between the natural and the supernatural. The Horseman closed the gate, locked them up behind it, and played warden. The deal was broken; the gates are open. Boom."

"I thought giving him back his stupid head would make the bargain go back into effect." Aimee's lips were pursed and she had the same expression on her face she got whenever she had to cram for a test. She could do the studying, but she never really liked it very much.

"No," Shane said. "All we did was give back what Crane took from him. It seemed pretty clear he was giving us a pass because of it, giving up on his vendetta. But that doesn't mean he's suddenly going to start corralling the monsters again. We broke the pact by coming back here." He shrugged. "Not like we had any way of knowing."

Aimee shook her head. "Whatever. As long as no one's trying to chop my head off."

"Yeah, except Adam Weiss is dead, thanks to whatever's in that cornfield. And then there're the drownings. They might not be anything unnatural,"

Shane said. "But they might be. We don't know yet."

"Well, until we do, I say we leave the drownings to the police."

Shane considered that for a moment before replying. "I guess. But I think we need to keep an eye on it. People don't drown in their own beds every day, and if it does turn out to be something . . . inhuman, it's not like the cops are just gonna guess that. I mean, the ordinary person doesn't find someone passed out with a couple of holes in their neck and automatically think 'vampire.'"

Aimee shuddered. "Unless you're us, and you've seen the things we've seen."

"No doubt," Stasia added. "Anyway, the thing is, if I'm right about these spirits, they aren't usually that harmful, just nuisances. And I think I'm on the right track, because they never did anything to the Ingalsby family. Just to anyone who walked into the family's cornfields and made a mess. If I'm right, all we have to do is tell them that they're released from their promise to protect the land and they'll go away."

"Just tell them to leave?" Aimee sounded doubtful.

"Well, we have to tell them the right way or it won't make any difference."

"What's the right way?" Shane had to make himself keep talking in order to avoid just staring at Stasia. She was still on his mind way too much, but this was the first time they'd actually had a sustained conversation since the kiss they'd shared the night Aimee's arm got broken. They'd had a brief exchange that night in the hospital, during which she had seemed to feel just as awkward as he had, and that was the end of that. His relationship with his sister could be difficult enough without him getting involved with Stasia, no matter how much he liked her. Anytime Shane started getting ideas in his head, he would remember what had happened the last time he had dated one of Aimee's friends. He also had to suppress the twinge of guilt he still felt about her getting her arm broken. If he and Stasia hadn't been snogging, maybe Aimee wouldn't have gotten hurt. Hell, she could have gotten killed. He should have never let his sister go running off on her own that night.

His mind had wandered, but Stasia's voice brought him back to the here and now.

"In this case I have to burn some sage and try to pronounce a few lines of Celtic. Which is like trying to speak pig Latin when you're stoned off your ass."

"Get Jekyll to do it. He seems to thrive on being stoned." Aimee rolled her eyes.

"Steve's a good guy, Aimee," Shane said. "I wouldn't be too quick to judge. Anyway, sounds like Stasia knows what she's talking about."

He tried to keep his tone light, but inside he

hated the thought of Stasia getting high. The difference between friendly acquaintance and girl he was obsessing over. If there ever was going to be something between them—not that there was, not after all the angsting he'd been doing about that very thing—he could handle her being a party hound but not a total burnout. She wasn't, but even the possibility got under his skin. Which was silly because they were just friends. Not even. He wasn't letting himself get that close. She was Aimee's friend.

Who are you kidding? he thought. But he didn't let his brain take those thoughts any further.

"I've indulged a time or two," Stasia said, shrugging. "It's not like a hobby or anything. And Jekyll likes to party, sure. But he never lets it get out of hand. His problem is he won't just give in to the party gods and dance. The boy just will not even try."

Thinking about Stasia dancing—and he'd heard a few stories from Jekyll and Hyde about the way she moved when she was in a dancing mood—made Shane's face get warm and forced him to shift the way he was standing to avoid embarrassment.

"Damn it," Aimee snapped, breaking him from his reverie.

"What?"

Aimee pointed at the field that was their main objective. There was nothing much to see. A few of the memorial pieces to Adam Weiss were still there, but everything else was gone. Sometime during the day Jim Ingalsby had gone ahead and harvested what was left of his crop. They could still see where the party had been—there was a lot of debris out in the field, just no corn.

A look of utter misery passed across Stasia's face. "Well, that sucks. Looks like the guardian spirits will have to wait until he gets a new batch of veggies planted."

"Cheer up, Stasia," Shane said. "There's still a tree we need to burn down." He meant it as a joke, sort of. They had plans for destroying the Whispering Tree, but they had to find it first. That seemed to be part of its magic. Either it moved or it made people forget exactly where they'd seen it. Whatever it was, Shane just wanted to be there when it burned. The very idea of the thing existing bothered him. Anything that lured people in with dark secrets and forecasts for a dismal future was bad enough, but when it tried to kill the people it drew in, there could be no justification for letting it stay around.

"Not today." Stasia shook her head and looked at her watch. "And not tonight, either. Aimee and I have places to be." She was smiling again, and Aimee joined in. Shane felt another twinge in his stomach. They were going out to party. "You want to come along, Shane?"

Shane thought about it for half a second and

then shook his head. He didn't need to be around when Stasia was having a good time dancing with other guys. He was being enough of a glutton for punishment even hanging with her when they went looking for the nasty little secrets lurking around Sleepy Hollow.

"Are you ever going to socialize, like, in your life?" Aimee asked, arching an eyebrow.

"Next time."

Stasia just shrugged. Shane's lack of wanting to be where the action was obviously wasn't going to take away from her fun and games. But Aimee couldn't resist getting in a quick jab. "See? I told you he wouldn't come. He's outlawed having fun."

CHAPTER
SIX

SHANE HAD GOTTEN home to a message on the answering machine from Steve Delisle. He was pleasantly surprised to find that whatever party Aimee and Stasia were going to, it was too small to be of interest to Jekyll and Hyde. So while his sister and her best friend were off having a good time, Shane hung out with the two mismatched guys who were as close as he'd gotten to making friends in the area.

They were at Jekyll's place, a house that looked like it was designed to seat a few hundred people comfortably. Stasia Traeger's family lived in an old colonial that was large but not overwhelming. Steve lived in a more modern home that was not only large but sat on enough land to hold a shopping mall. His parents did the Wall Street thing and they apparently did it very well. From what little Steve said about it, his father was one of the people who watched the movers and shakers of the business world do their stuff and played in the same fields, but with a little more caution. Whatever he was doing, Shane figured he was doing it right. Mark Hyde, on the other hand, claimed to live in a shack, but Shane figured that compared to Jekyll's house, just about anywhere could be considered a shack.

They were in the driveway, leaning against two different vehicles—a Mercedes and a BMW—and bouncing a basketball around. They had been shooting hoops in the backyard, where Steve's father had paved a small court and set up a backboard. Now they were resting, just tossing the ball to each other. It was something to do with their hands while they were going about the business of lamenting their miserable love lives. Shane had realized he needed to talk to someone about this obsession with Stasia that wouldn't quit. Get some perspective.

At the moment Steve was providing the perspective. "Shane, mi amigo, if you want to party with Stasia and you want to do more than party with her, just let Aimee know how you feel and get it done. The longer you wait, the worse it'll be if she ever finds out you two have feelings for each other." Sound, sage advice from the squirt.

Jekyll threw the basketball to him. Shane caught the ball and dribbled it for a few seconds. Then he shot it over to Mark, who caught it with one hand and held it in his grip.

"Looks good on paper," Shane said. "But you're forgetting that Stasia's been blowing me off ever since we kissed." He watched Mark bounce the ball off the tarmac a few times and then fire it at Jekyll like a missile. Steve caught it with a small grunt. "Besides, you don't know Aimee. There was a thing a couple of years ago when me and one of her friends in Boston sort of liked each other. It wasn't pretty."

"What? You dated the girl and then split up?" Hyde asked.

"This girl, Alyssa," Shane explained. "She liked me. We went out three, maybe four times. I didn't say anything and I guess Alyssa didn't either. Then she comes over one day and Aimee's all, like, 'Hey, what's up? Were we going to Newbury Street today?' But Alyssa was there to see me. I go out, we have a decent time, but when I get home, Aimee's in my face, freaking out on me for trying to steal her friend. Something about how we went behind her back and everything. She was crazy about it for months, and things were never really normal again with her and Alyssa."

"That seems a little . . . extreme." Hyde shook his head. "Tell your sister to grow up. You like Stasia, Stasia likes you." He shrugged. "Go for it, I say."

Jekyll snorted laughter. "Oh, yeah. Words of wisdom from the love machine."

Shane grinned at that.

Mark didn't. "Don't go there, Steve."

"Hey, I'm not the one who can't ask a girl out after three months, man." There was the strangest smile on Jekyll's face and a kind of amusement in his eyes, like he had some secret he wanted to share.

"If I could ever get her alone for five minutes, I'd ask her," Mark replied, a defensive edge to his voice.

Shane just watched in amazement. Jekyll was the only person he knew who would willingly rub Hyde's fur the wrong way. Half the teachers at the school seemed like they'd run if Mark decided to get bitchy. He didn't know if Coach Ferguson avoided Hyde because he was upset over Mark's refusal to play for him or because he was petrified, but he'd actually seen the coach spot the guy and then suddenly search for an alternate route.

"I'm going to find a way to get you two alone for ten minutes, Mark. I mean it. And when I do, and when you don't ask her out, I'm going to put an ad in the paper telling the whole town how you feel about her." Jekyll threw the ball in Shane's direction and Shane—who'd been far too busy watching Hyde's expression darken to notice much else—had to scramble to catch it.

"Let's get back on the subject at hand, which is Shane, not me." Hyde's deep voice was a rumble, his scowl more pronounced.

"What's the difference? You're both refusing to

do anything about the girls you're into." Steve shook his head, looking from one to the other. "Cowardice, I say. Absolute cowardice."

Shane dribbled the ball from one hand to the other and then threw it at the old basket behind the BMW—Mr. Delisle had put up the one in the backyard to prevent them bouncing basketballs off his car, but the old backboard was still up. Shane popped one off the rim and the ball bounced across the driveway, barely missing the car. Hyde caught it and lobbed the ball at Steve, who ducked and kept his smarmy smile firmly planted.

"I haven't seen you hanging with any models lately, Delisle," Hyde said.

Jekyll shook his head and laughed, that same mischievous glint in his eye. "As a matter of fact . . ."

Hyde scowled. "Oh, right."

Shane wasn't so quick to dismiss Steve's implication. Not with the smirk that he wore just then. "What are you saying?"

Jekyll threw up his hands. "Only that I am the king when it comes to attracting the ladies. I'm a magnet, boys. Seriously. I've been waiting for one of you goons to ask me what I was up to last night. You want to talk supermodels, Mark? I was hanging with three of them last night."

Hyde rolled his eyes. "I'm not talking about your favorite web sites."

"No, seriously. Well, *they* were hanging; I was just watching and enjoying. I'm just the luckiest guy in the world. Or at least in the Hollow."

"Yeah? Where was this?" If there were models hanging around, Shane figured he could use the distraction.

Jekyll was still smiling, but the expression had changed. Before, he'd been a guy with a secret, but now he was playing it coy, letting on that he'd been exaggerating. "All right, it may be that they didn't even know I was there—story of my life—but I did see them. The hottest girls I have ever seen in the flesh. And I'm talking *in the flesh*. They were skinny dipping last night in the river."

"Bullshit! In this weather?" Hyde scoffed. "You've been smoking something new."

"Well, I was smoking, but just the usual. Nothing exotic."

"Uh-huh." Hyde just stared at him.

"Where in the river?" Shane asked.

"Not far from the docks. I know a little place. Why? You hoping to score with some frozen cuties?"

Shane wondered how much of what he was thinking he should share. After a second he just went ahead and told them. "Hey, frozen or thawed, I'd be happy either way. But I was asking 'cause, well, there was this murder a few nights ago and a witness said he saw these naked girls leaving the scene."

"Come on." "No. Seriously. I heard about it when I was working. You should tell my dad where you saw them."

"Not a chance."

"Why not?"

"You weren't paying attention, were you? I was stoned. I don't want my parents figuring out where I go."

"Well, how about if I tell my dad about it?"

"Fine, but leave my name out."

"I can do that." He patted his pocket for a pen and paper and then cursed himself silently for not having his school bag with him. "Okay. Where did you say you saw them?"

"There's a little fishing place I used to go with my dad. About a quarter mile upriver from the docks. If you drive past the docks, there's an access road on the left, right past the old car plant, the one that's closed down?"

Shane nodded.

"Take that side road," Jekyll went on. "It dead-ends right up against the water. And Shane? Be gentle. It's still one of my favorite places to get wasted in peace."

"Deal. I'll try to keep it low-key."

"Cool. Well, listen, losers. You two can hang here and play ball if you want to, but I've got a date."

"A date?" Hyde asked, obviously dubious. "With?"

"Steffie Jenkins."

Shane had absolutely no idea who that was. Apparently neither did Hyde, who looked at his best friend with a blank expression.

"She goes to Irvington," Steve explained.

"Had to import one, huh?" Mark said.

"Maybe you should try it sometime."

Hyde shot him the finger, then turned toward Shane. "Sorry, man. I gotta take off too. Gotta go to work." He stretched. "So, Shane. There's a party this weekend. You're gonna be there, right?"

Shane looked at the giant in front of him. "I'll try."

"No. You'll be there." That was the end of the discussion as far as Hyde was concerned. He waved and headed on his way, walking down the long driveway.

Steve chuckled. "Dude. That's official. You're partying with us this weekend."

Shane nodded. "I'm getting that."

"Good. Terror works every time."

Alan Lancaster shot a dubious glance at Aimee and Stasia. "This just can't be exciting for you guys."

Aimee smiled, hoping it was convincing. "Dad, I never turn down extra credit. God knows I need all the help I can get. Besides, you're stressing about work all the time, but I never get to see what it's all for. It's kind of cool to watch you in action."

That one worked. Her dad stood a bit straighter and smiled. "I guess I'll buy that. Mostly the extra-credit part."

Stasia lifted one eyebrow and shrugged. "Maybe we'll get lucky and see a corpse."

Aimee's father sighed. "Now, that motivation I can believe." He rolled his eyes and ambled over to talk to the police chief again.

Behind him, in the river, three boats were searching the area. Her father had taken Shane's story about the naked women in the river very seriously, and so had the police. Obviously they were all pretty intent on the so-called drownings. Three women in the waters of the Hudson weren't a joke as far as they were concerned, but Shane had misled them all just a bit, claiming that the same friend who'd told him about seeing the women had claimed they had gone under and not come back up.

For his part, Shane was wandering around with his eyes downcast and a frown on his face. He was up to something, but she had no idea what. Stasia was scoping out the adults and doing her best not to be seen by Burroughs. That wasn't working. The police chief had given both girls a long stare, like he was waiting for some secret sign that they had done something illegal.

Stasia looked like she could think of a lot of places she'd rather be, and Aimee was with her on that. Her attitude changed a minute later when Shane came walking past, his frown more pronounced than before, and strode right up to their father.

"Dad? Have you looked at the edge of the river?"

"No. Something worth seeing other than mud?"

"Oh, yeah. It looks like somebody's dumping something they shouldn't."

Their father's expression was grave. "Show me."

Alan and Shane moved toward the water and Aimee and Stasia followed. Her brother pointed to a pipe that was spilling something nasty and greasy into the water, leaving behind a thick rainbow slick that was slowly dispersing.

A minute or so later the police chief was looking down at the same spot and scowling like a Chinese demon mask. "That's just what the Hudson needs."

"Safe to say that's illegal, Ed?"

"Well, unless they changed the rules around here, yes. Somebody's dumping a lot of waste that I'm betting hasn't been approved by the EPA." Ed Burroughs looked over at Shane and nodded, his face almost managing a smile of approval. "You've got a good eye, Shane."

"Somebody has to." Stasia said the words under her breath, and fortunately the police chief didn't hear her as he walked away, following along as Shane pointed out where he thought the pipeline was buried.

"Oh, you're a bitch when you want to be," Aimee said, arching an eyebrow.

"Only when I want to be? I have to work on that."

Shane walked back over to them, smiling like a good little Boy Scout. "Somebody's gonna get busted. I'd hate to be on the receiving end of the fines."

Aimee shook her head in disgust. "I'd like to find the loser who's behind the dumping and cut off vital parts of his anatomy."

Shane seemed surprised by her anger. He shrugged. "It happens all the time, Aimee. Whoever's responsible, Dad and the cops will drag them through the mud now. But it probably hasn't done much damage. Just flowing through such populated areas, the river gets polluted. It's inevitable. This sucks, but your solution might be a little extreme."

"What's too much damage, Shane? If it kills half the fish in the river or wipes out the water plants, is that too much?" They'd had similar arguments in the past. Sometimes she thought Shane took the opposite side of her opinions just for the pleasure of a good fight.

"You know, you always talk war on pollution, Aimee, but I've never once seen you actually take any action. If you're so bothered by this stuff, why aren't you out doing something about it?"

"Silly me. I thought that was what the government was for."

"Oh, come on. The government's too busy taking payoffs from these companies to do anything but look the other way. When this stuff gets out to the public, it's almost never some government report. It's people who care enough to do more than just complain about it."

He always knew the right buttons to push to piss her off.

"You know what, Shane? You lucked into something. That doesn't suddenly make you the great detective. As far as I'm concerned, the river is part of this town. That means the police should be looking out for this kind of thing. For that matter, what happened to good investigative reporting? The cops and the newspapers, they're supposed to be our watchdogs. Did you see anything on TV about this crap? I know I didn't."

"Like you're ever even home long enough to catch the news."

"Don't change the subject. You wanted to have a fight, well, here it is. As far as I'm concerned, the police dropped the ball. And since he's the major news source in town, I'd say Dad dropped the ball too. And with this attitude of yours, like, 'Hey, it's only a little illegal dumping,' you're only contributing to the problem. You might as well have spilled that stuff in the Hudson yourself for all you'd ever do to set it right." She wasn't quite yelling, but she was pissed off. If Shane wanted to go a few rounds, that was just fine with her.

Instead he held up his hands, looking disgusted. "Yeah, Aimee, you're absolutely right. I dug the pipeline and I hid it in the ground. I even hid it between the trees and camouflaged it with leaves. Me and Dad, we're in it together. It's really been me all this time, dropping God knows what in the river, and do you know why? Just to make sure you have a reason to bitch."

Stasia stepped between them. "Guys? I thought you were supposed to be trying not to fight. Truce, remember? Besides, you're drawing a crowd."

Aimee looked over and saw her father and Ed Burroughs staring in their direction. "Whatever." She shook her head. This was another fight between her and Shane that would have to be finished later. Which was just fine. She could wait.

Shane turned and walked away, shaking his head. Aimee watched him start back into the woods, his eyes tracking his new discovery like he was hoping to find gold.

"Stasia, why is my brother such an idiot?"

"I don't know about that. But for a smart guy, he sure spends a lot of time saying things that are just not very bright." Stasia shrugged and flipped her hair back, looking after Shane as he walked away. "Seriously, Aimee. What guys do you know that actually use their brains?"

"Not a one. Not a single solitary one."

"Sad, but true. They're cute, but stupid."

"Isn't that what they say about us?" Aimee made herself smile, determined not to let her brother ruin her mood.

"Yeah. But *they're* wrong."

"Good point."

In the darkness of the river, a few feet from the shore, something splashed noisily. When Aimee turned to look, she saw nothing unusual. She didn't give the sound any more thought.

She should have.

Mark Hyde pulled off one of his thick leather gloves and lit a cigarette. They were his guilty little secret. He didn't like them or the taste, but he loved the smell. They reminded him of when he was a kid and his dad was still around. Once he had the cigarette burning, he set it carefully against the remains of a car bumper and settled back to relax for a few minutes. It was cold as sin, but he was still sweating. Working with his uncle at the Sleepy Hollow Reclamation Center paid well, but the work was rough. Uncle Lloyd was cool with him taking a few breathers on the clock. He knew Mark wasn't sitting on his butt all the time. He worked hard, and now and then he had to rest. He didn't take advantage of the man. He knew better. There were plenty of people who could do the work and would be grateful for it. Just because his uncle ran the place didn't mean that he wouldn't get fired if he got sloppy.

One of the things Mark liked best about the job was that he could be alone with his thoughts while he worked. Steve Delisle was his best friend, but there were things he didn't tell Steve or anyone else and there were things he needed to resolve on his own.

When it had burned most of the way down to the filter, Mark crushed out the cigarette and tossed the butt into a pile of refuse after making very, very sure it was extinguished. He'd had to help put out three fires over the summer and didn't want to deal with any more.

The sun was going down low enough that he'd have to stop for the night soon anyway. There wasn't much he could do with the mountains of scrap metal around him in the dark except maybe get himself killed. Most of the metal in the heaps was from trashed cars and old appliances. Almost everything had edges, and even what didn't was heavy enough to break bones if it came down on top of him. His uncle was good about making sure the stacks were pretty stable, but there had been a few incidents in the past and Mark didn't relish the idea of becoming a statistic.

He started walking, heading back toward the narrow trailer that was his uncle's office. Lloyd had bugged out a little early. His wife was expecting a baby and it was almost time for Mark's new cousin to make an appearance outside the womb.

So Mark was alone when the sounds began.

He froze, knitting his brow as he glanced around. The hair on the back of his neck stood up. Metal didn't rest easily. Lloyd said it talked, and Mark knew exactly what he meant. The wind blowing through the mountains of steel caused whispers and moans, but the shifting of the metal in the stacks made a groaning, creaking sound that was unique in Mark's experience. Most of the time the sound was soft, a sort of counterpoint to the wind that you really didn't hear unless you were listening to it, like the chittering and squeaks of the rats that scoured the place looking for food or a good spot to nest.

When the metal started talking louder than that, it was time to get his ass out of the way. Mostly it meant something was going to slide, and if you were too close, you could find yourself pinned under half a ton of car or refrigerator.

But the metal hills around Mark weren't whispering tonight. They were talking loud and clear, especially over to his left. Mark moved a little faster, feeling a ball of tension form in the pit of his stomach. Uncle Lloyd did a great job of keeping everything as neat and orderly as possible, with wide trails between the towers of crushed steel and aluminum, but there were still some areas where it just wasn't wise to let down your guard.

Even in the gathering darkness Mark could see he was in just exactly the sort of spot best avoided when the metal got noisy. To his left, where the noise was worst, the pile of waste was topped with a stack of crushed gutters that had been banded together. If they decided to break apart from each other, the spot where he was walking was going to become a forest of sharp-edged trees.

As if on cue, it started to go.

"Oh, hell no." Mark ran, pouring on the speed as he heard the stack let out a whining metallic squeal. He cursed whenever his foot slipped in the oily slop that covered most of the trails and thanked God for each time he managed to keep his footing. Behind him the sounds of metal striking metal became as constant as the sounds of popcorn cooking in a microwave. He felt a few small pieces of debris bounce against his ankles and calves as he moved and prayed harder.

With an explosive roar the hill he'd been leaning against a few moments earlier became a wave of rushing recyclables, spilling across the junkyard and flattening anything that got in its way. The wave crashed into the shoreline of the next stack and took the base out from under it, starting a chain reaction. Mark didn't look behind him or bother trying to figure out where he would be safe. There was only one area in the entire yard that was safe from falling debris and that was Uncle Lloyd's office.

The cruddy little trailer had never looked better. Mark made it inside and pressed himself against the door. There was a loud crash and the entire trailer shifted a little, and then it was over. Quiet. No more falling junk.

Or it would have been quiet if not for Bonkers. The screech of metal, the general uproar, had set off the mastiff Mark's uncle kept around to protect the office. Bonkers was as sweet as sugar if he knew you and if Lloyd was around. Under any other circumstances he was a nightmare. Mark was the exception to that rule.

Tonight, though, Bonkers was just going nuts. The dog kept barking at the small window of the trailer, his hackles raised and every muscle tensed. Mark gave one try at convincing the animal to stop barking but gave up when Bonkers tried to remove his hand at the elbow. He decided to wait until the dog calmed down.

It was nearly an hour later that Bonkers was finally all barked out. The mastiff curled up below the window and continued to growl at it every few seconds, but the savagery that had overtaken the animal had subsided. When Mark left, he was careful to stay to the widest part of the trail as he walked. The place he'd paused to have a cigarette earlier was gone, buried beneath a few tons of debris.

He walked home, the same as always. Mark didn't have a car yet and wasn't really in a hurry to get one. But tonight he went a little faster than usual, his gaze darting from side to side as he walked, searching the darkest of shadows. He felt stupid and paranoid. The insanity at the junkyard had turned him into one big twitchy nerve. But knowing that didn't make him slow down at all.

Mark Hyde was used to being the one who made people skittish. Tonight, he knew how they felt.

CHAPTER SEVEN

THEY WORE GLOVES, heavy jumpsuits, and breathing filters. Their eyes were covered with protective goggles, and both Elizabeth Short and Deanna Crawford made a point of covering their heads with a vinyl wrap to avoid any staining or damage to their hair. Bill Winston wasn't as picky. What little hair he had left was just something growing on his head, and Deanna figured it wasn't really important to him. Then again, Bill was comfortably married and didn't actively go looking for members of the opposite sex to impress. Both of his coworkers were still single.

Their jobs at the Watson-Powell Research Laboratories required a great deal of knowledge about the manufacture of plastics and the willingness to work with potentially toxic by-products. They were careful. While most of what they worked with was stable and harmless, the polymers they were trying to design had already showed a certain penchant for caustic meltdown at temperatures over four hundred degrees. Aside from that little flaw, the team was exactly where they wanted to be on the project.

"Okay, stop. Stop. Stop!" Elizabeth wasn't known for her patience. She was screaming within half a second of the compound starting to slag. All three of them backed away from the cauldron where they were trying to work their magic and stared, disheartened.

"Hey, at least this time it lasted longer. . . ." Bill was always the optimist. "It's crap! This damned stuff is not working, people, and I want to know why."

Elizabeth was ready to rant and rave and Deanna really wasn't in the mood to hear it. She added water to their latest disaster and watched it break down again. Once the stuff had decided to fall apart, it did a very thorough job. Instead of a plastic as hard as concrete and as flexible as aluminum, they had a thick syrup that dispersed when it came into contact with regular tap water. This was not going well.

Bill turned off the flames under the test cauldron and then used the removable handle to dump the results into the drain below. None of them gave much thought to the drain. They knew it spilled into the Hudson somewhere down the line, but they had no idea exactly where. And as far as they were concerned, the dumping was perfectly safe. The toxins that came out were mostly water-soluble, and the ones that weren't would degrade in a few months. From time to time Bill made jokes about three-eyed fish, and once he'd even brought in a sticker showing a mutant fish from *The Simpsons*, but that was all just kidding around.

"Okay. So what haven't we tried as a bonding agent?" Deanna scratched her neck and felt the bands of tension under her skin. Mr. Powell wanted results and he was getting a little crabby about the whole affair. It would be time to look for a new job if they didn't succeed soon.

"I dunno . . . glue?"

"Ha ha, Bill. Deep inside, I'm laughing."

"Lighten up, Elizabeth. We're closer than we were; we just have to work out the fine details." Bill looked at the readouts from the sensors built into the oversized kettle, an oblong copper monstrosity capable of holding up to three hundred gallons of raw materials. "We got a lot closer this time. If we do this right, we're going to be very popular with the boss."

"And if we do it wrong, we're going to be very popular with the unemployment line." Deanna hated the whine in her own voice but couldn't help it.

"We still have time. It's just a matter of working out a few bugs." That was the thing about Bill: as far as his coworkers were concerned, he was their little cheerleader. He was also a great janitor. While they were debating what to do, he turned on the faucets at the sluice drain they used for their dumping and washed the last of the noxious substance down and away.

The three of them looked over the latest results, paying no attention to the running water or the drainage system. So they almost missed the sudden change. The fluids they'd washed down into the waste system came gurgling back up, bringing with them a renewed stench. The wet bubbling sounds alerted them to the problem and a second later the foul odors that came with the noises became woefully obvious.

"Oh, crap! Somebody get the mops." Elizabeth was in a full snit and Bill went for the plunger while Deanna went to grab their cleaning supplies. "God, guys, hurry up—this stuff is getting ready to geyser!"

"Come off it, Elizabeth," Bill said. "There isn't enough pressure from the river to make that happen." He was about to explain the physics of a drain system to her when the lights went out.

"Oh, this is just getting better and better." Deanna misjudged in the dark and almost blackened her own eye when she ran into the mop handle.

The darkness was almost complete. It would have been absolute if Bill weren't a smoker. He pulled out his lighter and flicked the small wheel, sending up a candle flame's worth of illumination. "Shouldn't we have emergency lights by now?"

"Maybe they forgot to check the batteries . . ." Deanna began. She thought she saw Elizabeth moving toward Bill in the darkness. Then she saw nothing at all as the lighter was slapped away from Bill's hand.

"Elizabeth? What are you doing?" She listened to the lighter skitter across the concrete floor and tried to concentrate on following the noise. The wet sloshing sounds emanating from the drain masked the Bic's final destination. "We're never going to find the stupid drain in this darkness."

"What do you mean? I didn't do anything." Elizabeth's voice came from entirely the wrong place. It sounded like she was over near the wall phone, which made sense since she was probably already dialing maintenance so she could do some more complaining.

Deanna frowned. If Elizabeth was over there . . . who had she seen with Bill? "Hey, Bill? Are you all right? You're awfully quiet." Maybe he'd slipped and fallen in the sludge rising from the sewer. Deanna knew he hated the dark. He'd freaked out the year before when the power went out in the long hallway and he'd had to find his way back to the lab by feel alone.

Bill didn't answer, but there was a sudden clatter

as the plunger he'd been holding fell to the ground. The wet noises from the drain were getting ridiculous now, and the stink was stomach-churning. Deanna imagined a fountain pouring back up from the drain, rising a couple of feet up from the center of the concrete depression.

"Bill? You okay?" He still didn't answer, but she heard a gasping sound from over by the phone. "Elizabeth? Liz?"

Deanna stretched out her hands, moving them in front of her body to make sure she didn't run into either of her coworkers. She didn't like their silence. It wasn't natural, especially for Elizabeth. Deanna's left hand brushed wet, bare skin and she heard a loud hiss come from whomever she'd touched. The flesh felt cold

Before she could say another word, she felt an impossible sensation. She was still standing, but it was like she had thrust her head into a bathtub. Water suddenly covered her face, like gravity had gone haywire and an ocean was floating above her. Terror lanced through her heart and her pulse beat wildly. Deanna tried to pull free, but the water followed her. She couldn't breathe and in the dark she couldn't see. The rest of her body was dry, but cold liquid covered her face completely, soaking her hair.

She reached up, her hands wet as they passed through the liquid. Panic raced through her like an electric shock. She stumbled in the dark, the need to breathe burning in her chest. Her foot caught on something and Deanna fell down, cracking her left knee on the edge of the concrete basin that was now overflowing into the room. The pain was so unexpected that she cried out, bubbles erupting from her mouth and stealing the last of the air in her lungs.

On her hands and knees now, Deanna tried to find something she could use to help her stand up again in the darkness. Her fingers grazed bare flesh. A woman. A naked woman with cold skin.

In despair and terror she inhaled, unable to resist any longer. Immediately the fluids filled her mouth, pushed into her throat, and forced her to gag and retch, even as her lungs spasmed against the harsh pressure of the liquids filling them.

Eventually Deanna's struggles ceased. She lay in the darkness next to her coworkers, her friends, unfeeling and unmoving. The water trickled slowly from her open mouth, and aside from that small noise the only sound was the wet sucking noise of water being pulled down the drain and spilled off toward the Hudson a quarter mile away.

Officer Dunfee stepped into the house, looking, like always, as if he was the man in charge. He wasn't—not by any stretch of the imagination—but Shane figured he liked to at least look the part.

Alan came out of the kitchen, his hands still damp from washing the dishes. Aimee had cooked—which wasn't nearly as disastrous as her brother normally made it out to be—and it was Shane's turn to handle the living room cleanup, so their father took a turn at the dishes.

"Tommy." Alan looked at the policeman. "Something wrong?" Both Aimee and Shane knew that the police officer was doing a little informing on the side, but Dunfee didn't know that they knew, though he might have suspected. Still, their father made it very, very clear that they were never to let on about that little tidbit. Good informants were hard to find, especially in a small town.

"No, just thought I'd check in and see how you folks were doing after the dust had settled."

Their father led the officer into the kitchen, offering him a cup of coffee. Aimee moved over to the open kitchen door, standing just beside it but out of sight, listening. Shane busied himself in the living room, pretending to be picking up backpacks and homework and pillows from the sofa. Instead he was playing lookout for his sister's eavesdropping. They were starting to get fairly good at sneaking around together. Shane could see his father's face as the officer spoke in soft words; Alan and Aimee wore similar pained expressions, so obviously the news wasn't good. Dunfee doused his coffee with more sugar than any human being should have been able to tolerate, then poured the contents of the mug down his throat. In less than a minute he said his goodbyes.

Alan waited in the kitchen until the officer had left and then walked back into the living room. "Okay, guys. Business before pleasure. There's been another situation with the drownings and I have to get myself down there."

"What happened this time?" Shane asked.

"Something pretty unpleasant, or so I gather. Down at a place called . . ." He consulted the napkin on which he'd hastily written his notes. "Watson-Powell Research, a plastics plant near where you found that pipe, Shane. It might even be the source of the contamination. They don't know yet."

"Think there might be a connection?" Shane asked. "You were talking about murder being about money, but maybe it's political. Like an ecoterrorist or something?"

Aimee made a face, but Shane ignored her. He wanted information, just in case it was something they had to look into.

Alan cocked his head as he started pulling on his jacket. "Anything is possible. Especially after this one. There are three victims, not just one. And it all happened inside their lab." He headed for the door, stopping to grab one of his cameras from the closet. "Either way, Ed Burroughs isn't getting out of this with evasive answers this time." He opened the door, letting in a blast of damp cold.

"Be careful, Dad." Aimee watched him, brows knitted with concern.

"I always am, honey." He stepped out and grabbed the doorknob. "Both of you be careful too. If you're going out, remember it's a school night. And I know you're curious, but don't go anywhere near the plant or the river, okay? No extra credit tonight. It sure sounds like we've got a killer with motive and not just some nutcase, but it pays to be careful."

He was gone a moment later.

Aimee picked up the phone, ready to dial. "Dad's glad it isn't some random thing, but in a way I wish it was. 'Cause I'm thinking you're right, that this has to be supernatural, and it's giving me the friggin' creeps."

"Yeah. Even if someone was tricky enough to drown someone and then move their body, doing it with three people at some laboratory somewhere . . . I'm not buying it."

"Exactly." She punched in the speed dial code and waited. "Hey. It's me. No, I'm not backing out. We're still on. I just wanted to see what you might know about a place called Watson-Powell."

Aimee was silent for a long while and then asked a few questions. Shane tuned her out, hating to hear only one side of a phone call.

He looked over his notes on the drownings, adding the name Watson-Powell and the number three. There had to be some kind of connection, but he couldn't imagine what a bunch of scientists would have in common with a painter, a night watchman, and a businessman who mostly seemed to work out of Manhattan. They obviously weren't running with the same crowd. As far as he could tell from what little he knew, they didn't even seem likely to know each other. Sleepy Hollow was small by Boston's standards, but there were still about ten thousand people in the town, and that meant a lot of different social groups. There was nothing to indicate that any of the previous three murders had connections. At least not so far.

Nothing except the way that they'd died.

Aimee hung up and turned back to Shane. "That was Stasia. You know her parents have that restaurant? Well, they've been catering the Christmas parties for Watson-Powell for as long as she can remember. She's still looking into it, but she thinks there might be some ties. That guy who drowned in his bed?"

"Perry Harper," Shane provided.

"That was it," Aimee agreed. "He was some big-deal executive with Watson-Powell. He was also a regular at the restaurant. That's a pretty big coincidence."

"Now we're getting somewhere." Shane walked over and sat down on the edge of the sofa, thinking hard. "Let's see what we have. Four people with the plastics place that is probably responsible for the dumping, a painter, and a night watchman. If we can figure out what the other two have to do with the ones from the plant, we might be on to something major."

"But not ecoterrorists?" Aimee smiled hopefully.

"I don't think so. Anything's possible, but it's too weird now. I think it's something else. Something monstrous."

Aimee nodded. "I think I'd prefer the ecoterrorists."

Alan Lancaster waited patiently at Watson-Powell for Burroughs to finish what he was doing and come talk to him. There was no reason to antagonize the police chief for the moment. There had been some tension, but that was part of the job. So far their relationship had been typical of what Alan had learned to expect from past experience between the press and the police.

That lasted another two minutes.

Burroughs strode over to Alan with a deep furrow creasing his forehead and eyes so rimmed with red that he looked like he hadn't slept in weeks. He was exhausted and he was obviously not at all pleased to see Alan. "What can I do for you tonight?"

Alan didn't hesitate. He had a job to do. "I heard

there had been an incident down here. Something about lab technicians drowning inside the building. I thought I'd see if you had any comments before I write the article."

Ed Burroughs sighed and rubbed his hand across his haggard face. "Only that I've found no connection to the other recent deaths."

"Oh, please." Alan flipped his notepad shut and looked at the man. "You're kidding, right?"

"No, Mr. Lancaster, I'm not." Mr. Lancaster. That wasn't a good sign.

"Chief, are you trying to tell me that you've had six unrelated drowning deaths in the last week? All but one of them away from water?" Alan shook his head. "That's about as unlikely as the notion that the Horseman killings were actually just a series of unfortunate shaving accidents."

"Now that's uncalled for, damn it."

"No, Chief. I don't think it's at all uncalled for. I have it on good authority that there are definite similarities in these murders—"

"Deaths. Not murders. That hasn't been determined yet."

"Okay, fine. Definite similarities in these deaths. Are you trying to say that my sources are making everything up?"

"I wouldn't know. Perhaps if you'd like to share your sources with me?"

"Maybe. Around the same time you start giving me the facts instead of the line you're feeding me now, we could possibly discuss where I'm getting my information."

"I'm not feeding you lines, buddy. I'm telling you the facts."

"You're telling me nothing. I could get more accurate information from a Magic 8-ball."

"This interview is over." Burroughs turned sharply on his heel and walked away, his hands clenched at his sides.

"Interview? Call me if you want to do one sometime, Chief. Meanwhile, I'll stick with the truth."

"You know something, Lancaster? You're a pain in my ass." Burroughs turned sharply and glowered at him. "The last thing I need around here is another reporter who thinks the crap he heard from his alleged sources is the gospel. I'm investigating a sensitive matter here and I don't need you leaking pertinent information before my investigations have been concluded."

"Then give me something I can use! I'm not quite a one-man show at the paper, but I might as well be. Part of my job is investigative reporting. I don't want to get in your way, but I do have a job to do. I'm not asking you to reveal everything you have, just enough to let me warn the public if there's a serious threat running around in Sleepy Hollow."

Burroughs tried to stare a hole through Alan's skull, but he wasn't willing to be intimidated. He'd run across tougher in Boston. A lot tougher. A few of them had left Alan doubting he'd live through the experiences. "Off the record?"

"If that's the way you want it." "Off the record, I think we're dealing with a nutcase who wants to make a political statement. There are some connections, but nothing I can say at the moment, because I don't want to scare off the perp. I want to catch the bastard and make him pay for what he's doing."

Alan considered his words before replying. "Fine. I can keep quiet about certain connections, Ed. But how do you want me to explain the three deaths here and the other drownings?"

"You can call these an industrial accident that's being investigated for possible criminal activities. But I don't want to hear about any connections to the other deaths right now. I don't want or need another media circus. I'm still dealing with the blowback from the Horseman killings. I'm not the top of the food chain, you know? I've got people to answer to."

Meaning the mayor and the town council were pressuring the chief to keep a lid on this, terrified any further bad press would kill the tourist trade they'd worked so hard over the past decade or so to nurture, with all of the Legend of Sleepy Hollow signs on the lampposts. The media frenzy over the

Horseman killings had been nasty, but if Alan's powers of observation were right, he believed that some perverse element in human nature had actually caused an upswing in tourism, making people aware of the town and the legend again, drawing attention. Connected to that old legend, it was probably easy for some people to think of it all as unreal or even fascinating. But something like this, more murders, that was too much. There was no interesting angle the media could spin off it. Just people who had been killed in gruesome, inexplicable ways. And this time of year? So much for the Halloween tourist boom in Sleepy Hollow if the story got out.

Alan tried not to let his frustration and disgust show. Maybe Burroughs was just doing his job, but Alan thought the people who ran the town ought to be more concerned with public safety than tourism. Still, he had to work with the chief.

"All right, Ed. I can go with that for now. It isn't that I don't understand your position. I just need to be able to let people know if they should be worrying. Do you have any solid leads so far?"

"Nothing I can discuss. The connections are tentative."

Alan nodded. "I'll leave them out for now." He stuck his hand out to the police chief. "Nothing about any possible connections that I find unless I pass it through you first, okay?"

"I appreciate that."

"Can you give me names and ages on the victims? I'll wait for you to notify next of kin, but we're both busy men. If I can get the information early on, I can have the article ready to go when you give the all clear."

Ed Burroughs sighed and shook his head. "Yeah. But if it's in the paper before then, I'm not going to be happy."

"Trust me, Ed. I may not like the way things are going on this, but I'll play ball if I know the reason why and as long as it's not putting anyone in danger. Just understand that when the picture clears up for you some, I will report on it."

"Understood," the chief said. "We both have jobs to do."

When their dad came in after almost two hours, Aimee and Shane were engrossed in a heavy discussion about Perry Harper, Watson-Powell, and the drownings. Stasia had walked over to join them, which was fine with Aimee. Spending too much time alone with Shane normally resulted in another argument. But he'd decided to behave himself tonight and was sitting on an armchair and taking notes.

"Learn anything interesting?" Aimee leaned back against the base of the sofa, her feet under the coffee table. Stasia was sitting behind her, taking up most of the sofa, but she sat up and slid over as soon as she saw Alan.

He took off his coat and put it onto the rack as he walked closer to their gathering. "Oh, I'm getting quite an education in the way things are done around here."

Shane cocked his head. "You're not going to drop a line like that on us and then clam up, Dad."

Alan glanced at Stasia, obviously unsure what he should be discussing in front of her. Aimee waved a hand in the air to dispel his concerns.

"Please, Dad. Stasia is totally in the loop. I'm just going to tell her whatever you say later anyway."

That ruffled him. "I'm not sure I like the idea of you taking what I say around the house back to school with you."

"No worries, Mr. Lancaster. Seriously," Stasia told him. "Aimee and I talk about everything. That doesn't mean she's telling the world. I'm a pretty good judge about what is and isn't private conversation."

Alan shook his head, smiling in bemusement as he looked at Aimee. Then he sat down on the sofa near Stasia. "All right. What'd I learn? Only that Ed Burroughs is a lousy liar. He tried telling me that there were no connections between any of the deaths. I got him to admit there are connections, but

117

he's stonewalling for now. I think he wants the thing wrapped up with a bow before it really gets out so his bosses can figure out how to do damage control first."

Aimee smiled too. "He better work fast, then. Stasia has all the dirt on Watson-Powell."

"Really?" Alan leaned back. "Tell me everything and I'll buy you a pizza."

Stasia laughed good-naturedly. "How can I resist an offer like that?" She pointed to Shane. "He's got notes, but basically Perry Harper used to come into my parents' restaurant at least once a month. He set up all sorts of parties and stuff for Watson-Powell and was always bringing clients around for lunch or dinner." She shrugged. "He's not the big boss, but he was one of them at the place. The guy in charge actually has the last name of Powell. If there's a Watson, I never met him or heard my folks talk about him."

"Ed said there was a connection after I grilled him for a bit, but he didn't say what sort. So we know that four of these people worked for the same company. What we don't know is how the other two, Roberto Rodriguez and Gary Barnes, fit into this."

Shane sat forward, shooting his father an intense look. "Well, maybe it *is* something environmental. I was half kidding about ecoterrorists, but now I don't know. Didn't you say something about the house-painter dumping cans in the river?"

Alan nodded. "There was evidence that he might have been dumping his leftovers. Paint along the shoreline that was still wet. That's illegal because the stuff is toxic, obviously. But that doesn't explain Rodriguez. Or how whoever's doing it is managing it. I can see how some psycho wanting to send a message about not polluting the river could get the crazy idea that drowning people would get the point across, but the Harper killing left no extra water around. Not on the bed or the carpet. I suppose some of it could have dried, but . . . it's an awful lot of work to drown someone in a sink or a bathtub and then . . ." He scowled. "Damn. I shouldn't be talking to you guys about all this horrible stuff. I'm sorry."

"No, Dad, it's okay," Shane said. "We want to help. You need someone to bounce things off, and, well—"

"It *is* sort of fascinating," Aimee added.

He shrugged. "I suppose. But the last thing I want is to give you any more material for nightmares."

Shane scoffed. "We're not kids, Dad. We can deal."

Alan grinned. "I keep forgetting. Anyway, I'm still thinking this might just be someone with a grudge against Watson-Powell. Maybe it's something as easy as a disgruntled ex-employee. A whistle-blower scenario."

"Could be Rodriguez was covering for them,"

Stasia put in. "Watson-Powell, I mean. He was, like, the guard or whatever down at the docks, right?"

"I'll have to look into that. I think I saw something about him having a tour boat on the river. Maybe he saw something he wasn't supposed to or caught whoever's been doing this when they weren't expecting to be seen."

Aimee shook her head. "Maybe he just drowned. I mean, he was in the water, wasn't he? At least part of the way? That doesn't sound like all of the others."

"True." Alan nodded. "The timing is pretty coincidental, but we can't assume that anyone who drowns is connected unless there's a visible trail. On the other hand, it never hurts to be thorough."

Alan kept his word. He ordered two pizzas. They talked more while they waited, the conversation turning into a debate. Before it was over, Aimee was discussing the general pollution problems and asked her dad to do a story on the condition of the Hudson River.

"If an ecoterrorist is doing this, maybe there's something to be worried about. Aside from a nut with a vendetta, I mean. When was the last time anyone checked the water in the Hudson for dangerous contamination?"

"Well, the Parks and Recreation Department checks the rivers and streams regularly. Haven't you ever seen those little caution signs? They test the water almost every day, and if the levels of *E. coli* are too high, they put up warnings. But I don't know what else they test for." Alan reached for another slice of pepperoni pizza and smiled at Aimee. "I'll look into it, honey. When I find out something, maybe we can sketch out an article together, as long as you remember it's an article, not an editorial."

"You know, if the water's really nasty, maybe you *should* let Aimee do an editorial," Stasia said. "It'd be nice to have one in the paper that didn't just cover whether or not we need a traffic light on Sullivan Street."

"Well, we do need a traffic light there," he said, "but you've got a good point. When we look into this, if you want to do an editorial, Aim, I'm all for it."

Aimee blanched at the idea. It was one thing to talk and another to actually have to write a paper. It was like schoolwork without the grade. But she really did hate what people did to the environment without ever thinking about the consequences.

"I'm up for it, Dad. Just give me a week or so."

"Done deal."

It was late when they were done, and Alan and Aimee gave Stasia a lift back to her house. Shane stayed behind, quieter than usual. He had something on his mind, Aimee was sure, but nothing he wanted to share with her. That was his decision and she wasn't going to force it. Her brother liked to bottle everything inside. She figured it was his ulcer to have, not hers. She was already anxious enough, knowing what the three had planned for the next day.

CHAPTER
EIGHT

THE NEXT MORNING was overcast and damp. There hadn't been any rain as far as Aimee could tell, but the ground was soaked with morning dew. She was filled with the same dread she felt every time they went off looking for the Whispering Tree. The encounter she and Stasia had had with the tree still haunted her. She got shivers when she thought about how the tree had dug into her mind and told her things she didn't want to know or hear. The monster had been attacking her only real friend in town—the girl who was pretty much her best friend now—and Aimee had jumped in to defend her. They had managed to escape, so she couldn't be sure what the tree was after, but there was a big hole in its trunk and it had sure seemed like the tree was going to try to *eat* them.

It should have sounded funny. Instead it made her want to run and hide. All in all, she would rather have been cleaning toilets at the Capitol Theatre.

Too bad the new job didn't start until next week.

On the other hand, Stasia actually seemed *eager* to run across the nightmare tree again. Shane, who had never seen it at all, was dying to see it too—he was itching to burn it to the ground. He carried a two-gallon gas can with him every time they made this trip, hoping to torch it before it could kill anyone.

Every town had someone go missing from time to time. Runaways. Loners who drifted off or skipped out on their rent. But maybe there wasn't an easy explanation for some of them. There were a handful of people who claimed to have seen the tree, heard its unpleasant whispers, but Aimee wondered if the thing had done more than talk, if it had killed anyone. Eaten anyone. The thought shivered through her body along with a low moan of wind cutting through the trees.

"Okay, didn't we cover this area last week?" Shane's voice was a bit strained. He acted like the gas can wasn't heavy, and maybe it hadn't been at first, but after half an hour or so of lugging it around, he was sounding a bit out of wind.

"Yes, we did. We're going farther this time. And if it really moves . . ." Aimee didn't continue. She didn't have to. They all knew the stories.

"There!" Stasia jumped and pointed. "That spot. I remember that stump."

"A stump?" Shane sounded dubious.

"Yeah." Stasia looked at him, her face bright and smiling. "It looks like Coach Ferguson."

Shane looked at the remains of a tree that must have been downed by bad weather years before and squinted. "Yeah. I can see that. Has the same profile."

"Exactly!" Stasia traced it with her finger, emphasizing the lines she thought made up the coach's face.

Aimee still didn't see it. "You're being weird. Let's just find the tree and get this done."

"No sense of adventure, Aimee. Quit strangling your inner child." Stasia raced ahead, and Aimee envied her friend's courage.

They looked around, Aimee watching her brother and Stasia as they looked at the local flora, searching for her nightmare. She wasn't having a good time and couldn't understand how either of them could get so excited about what they were doing.

It's a monster. They don't get it. It works into your head and screws with your mind! This isn't a game, damn it, and they keep acting like they're searching for buried treasure.

She kicked at a loose clump of dirt and her foot slammed into a root. Aimee looked more closely at the root, at the weeds around it. There was a hole in the ground, deep and moist. One thick shoot stuck out of that pit, broken and bleeding a deep red sap. She'd seen that color liquid spill out of a tree only once in her life and that had been when she'd broken a thick branch on the Whispering Tree.

For a second she couldn't breathe. Her mind had to grasp the implications and it seemed to take everything she had to make the idea small enough to hold on to.

"Guys." She waited for a response but didn't get one immediately. "Guys! I think I found it!"

Stasia and Shane came running. Her brother was wide-eyed with what seemed like a combination of fear and excitement. Stasia was a bit slower than Shane, and she blinked in confusion when she got to Aimee.

"I'm pretty sure it was bigger than that, Aimee."

Aimee rolled her eyes. "I don't think it's here anymore. I think it's gone." Her voice sounded tinny.

"Gone?"

"Yeah. Look." She pointed to the red bleeding sap spilling from the root where it broke out of the ground. "I think someone took it."

"Who the hell takes a tree?" Shane looked from the hole they now surrounded to the tall dying grass around them. "I don't see any marks from a bulldozer or anything."

Stasia frowned and looked around. Aimee was

still focused on the drooling spill of bloodred sap dripping into the pit where the tree had been. It made her think of the socket left after a tooth was knocked out. The ground was loose and broken, the remaining fragment of the tree raw and bleeding.

"There's nothing," Shane said. "Maybe it really can move."

Aimee shook her head. "Not like that. It wouldn't move itself and tear a root away. That would be like cutting off your own foot when you decided to take a walk."

"Well, if it didn't move itself, what happened to it?" Shane scowled. He wasn't angry; he was thinking. Sometimes the look was exactly the same for him.

"Shane, that was a big tree. I mean *big*. Like a couple of tons of wood." Stasia walked back over to look into the wound where the tree had been. "If something else came along and moved it, there would be evidence."

"Let's get out of here." Aimee backed away from the spot, a feeling of deep, cold dread filling her stomach. "Whatever happened to the tree, it's gone, and if something did come around here that was big enough to haul that thing away, I don't want to be here if it decides to come back."

Aimee started walking back the way they'd come. She didn't know which bothered her more, the tree being missing without her knowing where it was now or the thought of what could have taken it. A moment later Stasia was walking by her side. Shane followed soon after, pausing only long enough to take a chunk of the root from where it lay and to wrap it in a scrap of paper he'd found in his pocket.

They took a different route on the way back. Stasia wanted to search the area, just in case the tree had relocated itself. They found no sign that an oak tree had recently torn itself from the ground and ambled down the hill on its merry way to parts unknown. But as they trudged through the heavy autumn vegetation, they came across a small park. The area was well kept, neatly groomed, and absolutely deserted on the cold morning. There was a small copse of trees around the pond, and even on the brightest days the small body of water would probably be heavily shaded. With the overcast sky getting darker, not lighter, there was little light at all that touched the surface.

Which made what they saw all the more unsettling. There was a boy out on the water, gliding smoothly along on a pair of ancient-looking ice skates. He wasn't doing anything spectacular, but his round face was filled with delight and his hair—showing under a hat that seemed plucked from *Oliver Twist*—whipped around behind him. He wore a long, thick scarf and a gray woolen jacket with big black buttons that reminded Aimee of pictures she'd seen of nineteenth-century immigrants coming to America through Ellis Island.

The three of them stood side by side, staring out at the ghost skating across the surface of the unfrozen pond. Aimee couldn't breathe. She was terrified, but that wasn't all. There was something achingly sad about watching the boy that made her chest hurt.

"Do kids usually ice-skate without ice around here?" Shane whispered, glancing over at Stasia. He was kidding, but there wasn't a trace of amusement in his face. His eyes were wide and this time Aimee could read the expression in them easily—it was the same fear and sadness that she felt in her own heart.

Out on the pond, the ghost was laughing and skating, his sweet face looking up at someone taller than him and his hand held out, beckoning to someone who wasn't there and was probably as dead as he was. She shivered again, wishing that ghosts were still just in movies and books instead of a part of her world.

A moment later a break in the clouds let in a glimpse of blue sky and a shaft of sunlight that fell upon the woods and the pond, and the boy was gone.

Aimee felt Stasia's arm wrap around her shoulders. "Come on. Let's go see what's up at the

Capitol. Maybe we can get a schedule so we can actually work, you know, to make money?"

"Yeah," Aimee agreed. "Beats looking for trees."

Stasia looked back to where they'd found the hole in the ground earlier. Her smile faded a bit. "Yeah. Well, at least that's over with, right?"

"Let's hope." Shane rubbed at his eyes and looked out at the pond again. Then he turned away and started toward home.

Aimee and Stasia followed. Behind them the pond was calm and quiet. They weren't there to hear the happy sounds of a little boy laughing or to hear the same boy's voice later when the ghost began to scream.

Shane leaned against the old chain-link fence near the docks and stared out at the water. He'd had a busy day and wanted to get everything done before the sun had completely set. Naturally, it wasn't working out that way.

At least he had Jekyll and Hyde helping him, sort of. Steve was pretty good on the whole research thing when he put his mind to it, and after Shane promised to join the two of them at the next party they attended—like he'd risk Hyde ripping his arms off—Jekyll had promised to look into Watson-Powell. It was cool that Stasia had dug up the information she had found, but they needed more than just who had eaten at the Traegers' restaurant.

Meanwhile, Mark was going to see what his uncle knew about the painter and the night watchman. Lloyd Hyde was a blue-collar guy with a fondness for dives like the Setback Inn. According to his nephew, Lloyd had known Gary Barnes from "around."

Now there was one last task—this one for his father, though he had no idea Shane was doing it— and then Shane would head home. Alan was dashing around like a maniac, attending to the usual business of running the paper and trying to be a good reporter, which meant investigating Watson-Powell. Shane figured his dad would probably get around to it eventually, but Alan had a lot on his plate, and dealing with the illegal chemical spillage was something Shane could help out with easily enough. He had decided to swing by the riverfront and collect a few samples from the pipeline he'd found and from the water around it. Two cleaned-out mayonnaise jars and a couple of Ziploc bags later he was on his way.

He moved upstream, leaving his fence and resting spot behind. He made his way through the light woods, enjoying the relative peace, and eventually he found the clearing where Steve Delisle liked to mellow out and where the pollutants dripped from a pipe in the ground. He'd followed the drainage system as far as he could through the woods the other day, surprised by how easy it was to track the underground system until the layout of the land changed and suddenly it plunged deeper into the earth. Still, he could look even now and see the building that he knew was part of Watson-Powell's property. All he had to do was track with his eyes from where the pipe disappeared into the ground and he could make out a straight line to the squat, industrial structure.

Ed Burroughs had said he'd look into it. What was taking so long, when the problem was this obvious? Shane wondered if the cops had to have some kind of warrant or something to dig. Or if maybe Burroughs really was just completely stonewalling.

Shane opened his first jar and set the lid in his jacket pocket. A light splash came from the water and he glanced out at it but saw nothing out of the ordinary. Even so, he shivered and wished Aimee and Stasia were there. No matter how much Aimee sometimes got on his nerves, he decided just then that her company would be better than being alone here. Not to mention Stasia's company. He shook his head. Best not to think about Stasia.

Every time he thought he might be getting to understand the girl, she pulled a fast change. Her hair was never the same color for very long—the highlights, at least, which this week were a light honey blond—and she changed her fashion sense and her makeup just as often. The only constant lately was that she was cool around him whenever Aimee was there and made a point of avoiding him when Aimee wasn't.

The first jar was filled with a few inches of the thick slop that had coagulated around the edge of the pipe. He had to lean out over the water to collect the sludge, and what he got on his hand felt wet and cold and greasy. Shane sealed the jar and carefully set it on the ground. Aimee would be so proud, no spills.

He opened the other jar and leaned out over the water, sticking his hand deep into the Hudson to make sure that the sample he drew in wasn't just from the surface. When the last bubbles had been emptied out and the container was full, he lifted it out of the water and reached for the lid, balancing carefully on his knees. The last thing he wanted to do was go for an accidental swim.

He was shaking the last drops of excess from the sealed sample and stepping back from the river when she came out of the water, her dark hair cascading down over her shoulders, her eyes wide and innocent and stunningly blue. Her face was heart-shaped, with delicate features, and even without makeup she could easily have passed for a model. The expression she wore was all that marred her perfection. Her teeth were bared in an animalistic snarl of rage and her eyes narrowed in hatred as she rose higher from the water, her flawless body unclothed. Shane was so shocked he couldn't move. Delicate hands grabbed him, changing as they touched his body. Long fingers with wicked claws snagged his coat and he felt the fabric tear even as he was pulled down into the river.

Cold, filthy water flowed around his face and neck and Shane felt himself pulled deeper beneath the Hudson. Disoriented, he tried to scream. The air spilled out of his lungs, the bubbles of his breath swirling away into the darkness. His heart thundered with fear. Panicked, Shane tried to keep his eyes open to see where the bubbles went because they could lead him to the surface, but she had ahold of him and was pulling harder, dragging him down and away.

He kicked out and felt his foot connect with a solid form. Maybe the ground, but he didn't think so. It was too dark and the thing that had its hand on him was pulling him through the water, twisting him around and keeping him disoriented.

His lungs felt like they were being crushed in a vise and the frigid water chilled him, making his muscles sluggish. Shane kicked out again, felt something shift where he'd planted his foot, and pushed as hard as he could. The woman—or whatever she was—eased off for a second and Shane twisted, trying to get free. The fabric of his coat ripped even more, and he felt the pressure that was pulling him